A BLESSING IN DISGUISE

A Blessing in Disguise
Edited & Compiled by Pravallika Kadiri
Print Edition

First Published in India in 2021
Inkfeathers Publishing
New Delhi 110095

ISBN 978-81-950205-2-2

www.inkfeathers.com

A BLESSING IN DISGUISE

Edited & Compiled by

Pravallika Kadiri

Inkfeathers Publishing

DISCLAIMER

The anthology "A Blessing In Disguise" is a collection of 19 stories by 18 authors who belong to different parts of the globe. The anthology editor and the publisher have edited the content provided by the co-authors to enhance the experience for readers and make it free of plagiarism as much as possible. Unless otherwise indicated, all the names, characters, objects, businesses, places, events, incidents- whether physical/non-physical, real/unreal, tangible/ intangible in whatsoever description used in this book are either the product of the author's imagination or used in a fictitious manner. Any resemblance to actual persons, objects, entities, living or dead, or actual events is purely coincidental. The stories published in this book are solely owned by their respective authors and are no way intended to hurt anyone's religious, political, spiritual, brand, personal or fanatic beliefs and/or faith, whatsoever.

In case, any sort of plagiarism is detected in the stories within this anthology or in case of any complaints or grievances or objections, neither the anthology editor, nor the publisher are to be held responsible for any such claims. The author(s) who holds the rights to the story, shall be held responsible, whatsoever.

CO-AUTHORS

Sankalp Nanda, Aditi Agarwal, Raghavi Shankara Guhan, Aashreya R, Aashritha Kadiri, Anoushka Sharma, Archana Natarajan, Prajwal Shukla, Naqiyyah Calcuttawala, Malvica Sangeetham, Hitesh Kumar Singh, Akshaya Kosuri, Deepshikha B, Likhitha Kotika, Lakshmi Sai Kumar, Sucharan Reddy, Harshit Dudhani, Jerry Akshita

CONTENTS

ABOUT THE EDITOR

Pravallika Kadiri

Pravallika is a 20-year-old management student who likes to put her thoughts on a paper rather than her mind either by writing or painting. She believes that art has the power to heal people and she also believes that everything in this universe happens for a reason and you reading this right now might have a reason too. Lastly, she is someone who knows how to see a rainbow even in the dark, just by holding onto that one beam of light she finds!

You can connect with her on Instagram @pravallika_kadiri and you can find her paintings which are a happy escape for her @artlykay.

EDITOR'S NOTE

I've always wondered what would happen if life was all about happiness. Would we feel wretched about being happy all the time or would we still be happy about it?

We have all gone through situations that we didn't want to be in. We have all gone haywire about why life was throwing us in a place we never wanted to go. But, have you ever seen a blessing in disguise in such situations? Or have you realized after a few years about what good has come out of it and everything made sense then?

I always believe in the fact that EVERYTHING HAPPENS FOR A REASON! And there will definitely be a blessing that one can find in disguise! It is all about how you find it!

And before you start thinking that I'm just being all positive about life.. No! I'm not being all positive about life! It is just that we all have been running behind things so much that we have left behind a simple fact of life that everything happens for a reason!

It's strange how believing in some simple sentence changes the way one can look at life!

Keeping that in mind, I've compiled this book with the 19 best stories that revolve around finding blessings in disguise. I've left a few pages for you to write down your story/incidence of blessing in disguise as the 20th story of the book. I'm sure that you have one or more stories as such! Just write down and you'll definitely feel different about it! And I'm also sure that each story that you read will be a different ride. A ride that might sometimes remind you of your own situations, a ride that might help you someday, a ride that might make you realize something that you've been ignoring all the while, a ride that might make you feel nice or a ride that you might just love!

Whatever this ride might make you feel like, I just hope that you enjoy it!

Happy Journey!

Pravallika Kadiri

A BLESSING IN DISGUISE

1

ALL OR NOTHING

by Sankalp Nanda

The image was still in my eyes- Vikas & I were sitting in the temple beside the fire, smiling cutely at each other. We were telling ourselves; this was a relationship of seven more *janams* (births). And yet, within 7 years, we collapsed like a house of cards, pointing out mistakes, trying to win every small battle till we reached a point where there were none left. My heart was still broken as I swiped photos left and right on a dating app. I didn't expect any more to meet the love of my life- I had met and lost him. I expected to meet someone with whom I could spend enough years for my parents to be happy. More importantly, I was hoping against hope to find someone who will talk and drown my sadness in the flood of his own happiness. It was all or nothing as I walked that day to meet Sarath. I knew if it didn't work out, I wouldn't have the courage to try it again for another year. But at the same time, I went in half hoping it didn't. Because my heart didn't have the space to let in someone new, and my mind didn't have the patience to try to learn about someone, his behaviour, and habits.

We sat in a quaint, little French restaurant with white and blue walls. I looked at Sarath properly only after 5 minutes of him arriving. I wonder what he was thinking about me till then. He asked me what I did, I said I was a writer. He seemed interested which wasn't unusual considering this was our first date. After 15 minutes of mundane conversation during which I had looked at him only twice, he asked me something that stopped my heart for a minute. "What did you come expecting from our meeting?" he asked me directly. I was taken aback and stared at him for a moment beyond the usual glance. I stuttered a bit; I was so confused whether I should open my heart to the first person I met after Vikas. I almost cried, trying to answer the question. He could read my face, I could feel it. He said, "Ok, why don't we start with something light. Tell me your favourite colour instead," and he smiled for a while. I laughed in my tears and laughed a bit more and said it was green. I told him the story about how I was asked to colour the leaves as a child for admission into a pre-nursery school, my parents had not 'prepared' me yet about entrance exams and I ended up colouring leaves with all the colours available. That funny story kept getting retold in my family & that's how my affinity for green began. I remember Sarath laughing so much at this story, I thought he would pass out. I caught a glimpse of his honest laugh and the beautiful smile around it and for a moment, it felt good. It is nice to surround yourself with happy people sometimes, they alleviate your pain and make you forget things- Things you want to forget but just can't.

I was drifting away in my thoughts when Sarath jumped in again with another one of his funny quips. "What's your favourite cartoon character?" he asked me. As I told him about Rugrats, he really had his mouth open. The next ten minutes were him trying to convince me that he really loved Rugrats & was not telling this 'only' to impress me. I did a quick-fire round on the characters, Tommy, Chuckie & my favourite Angelica. Boy, did he pass! Sarath said while had forgotten about it, he recently went on a nostalgic trip re-watching many episodes. I was chuckling by now; this was so much my habit.

Being a foodie, I had pretty much already decided the menu for our dinner. I wanted to show off fancy items I had read about in some good reviews. Sarath complied, without much choice, I must add here! I ordered a Baked Spaetzle with Green Pea Pesto & a Greek Salad (whose name I can't remember). I was very excited to try these new items and I think I went bla-bla about some of the reviews around it. Sarath just smiled, he wasn't a fan of continental food, I could tell, but he said he was always a Pasta lover (as white a lie as the white pasta we could have eaten).

After a wait of 10 minutes, our food arrived, and we dug in faster. I don't remember talking much as I loved the food and kept my focus completely on it. But after a few minutes, I lifted my eyes up. To my surprise, Sarath was not eating much, he was smiling & looking at me. I smiled back & asked him if he liked his food, he nodded back. I continued my tryst with good food and honestly, had the waiter not come back asking for any further order, I would have I guess remained deep in my love for food. When I looked at the watch, three hours had passed away breezily. With a slightly heavy heart, I smiled & then I told Sarath, "The next time we meet, maybe I can answer your first question." To which he replied, "So, you are sure we are meeting me again." His smile made me laugh like the last year never happened. I bid him goodbye and thanked him for the wonderful evening. In a sense, it was ethereal, but I didn't want to tell him yet. I refused Sarath's offer of dropping me home, in fact I waited for him to leave before starting my walk home. I have always been a fan of long walks in the midst of confusion, for me it always gave me a sort of clarity. As a writer, having a muddled mind never helps, I remember my post marital years as one of my worst creative ones. I stopped trying to write my long-fantasised novel. I just had nothing inside of me that helped me imagine/create. All I could write was sad thoughts about life, about the gray areas of relationships & struggles of modern-day couples. Initially, I used it to my advantage writing weekly columns in new age magazines. Soon, I felt my health suffered with all the negativity and I took a break. I guess it hurt Vikas more, I had put a lot of financial pressure on him without discussing with him & he struggled to deal with it. It kept making things worse. As my thoughts meandered towards Vikas and our marriage, I was feeling a bit uneasy. I looked ahead & I was crossing the yellow tainted streets with the backdrop of an orange sky. It felt beautiful & I felt happy. I was reminded of my beautiful evening with Sarath. "Could he be the one", I kind of asked myself. I was not ready for the answer though. I did not want to give him any benefit of doubt at all. I wanted to be strict with him, I wanted to evaluate him for years till I said yes, even though I felt like I wanted to. I walked till my feet hurt and then promptly, took an auto back home.

I was prepared for an early sleep tonight, "It will be a nice sleep after a long time." Just as my mind was feeling comfortable, I went back to the discomfort of relationships. Within seconds, I felt claustrophobic and asked myself why I was taking this risk again. Vikas was always a good human being, he had all the qualities I liked. My parents loved him and thought I was lucky to have him and here I am, within a few years, having to sleep alone on a small bed in a rented 1 BHK rather than trying to get my imaginary child to sleep. I was restless as I jostled around Sarath's question, "What did you come expecting from our meeting. "

I was asking myself, what was it exactly I was looking for. Was it love that I wanted to seek again because last time I received it; I ran as far as I could? Was it a solution for loneliness- because I was used to it, in fact I loved my loneliness, I loved all the quirky habits I had developed over the last year. Be it going for a late-night Maggi, the untimely walks around my apartment, the re-watching of my favourite sad songs on You Tube (worse crooning to it) and horrible voice to all those sad songs, especially All I Want from Kodaline) I knew it was time for a late-night walk, I pulled out my sneakers, got ready within minutes and just as I was about to open the door, my phone made a vibrating sound.

This wasn't something I was ready for. My heart started beating faster than earlier as I saw Sarath's name. I took a small breath before finally reading the message, It said, *"I'LL NEVER FALL IN LOVE AGAIN! AT LEAST NOT UNTIL THE FIRST GRADE."* This was a famous line of Angelica, I laughed on reading it and I must have read it at least a hundred times before finally going to sleep. I did not need a walk that night & after a long-long time, I went to sleep feeling light, feeling a weight had been lifted off my shoulders, off my mind. More importantly, I knew I had reached the First Grade.

2

ALL'S RIGHT WITH THE WORLD

by Aditi Agarwal

She had a good life. She taught you a lot." My aunt said, staring into my eyes earnestly, taking my hand in hers caressing my thumb. I nodded and gave her the smallest hint of a smile. I passed along all the guests, trying not to catch their eyes, so full of pity for the motherless child. There were so many promises of keeping in touch made, so many reassurances of being there for me were given, and sympathetic, pitiful looks were exchanged every time they thought I was looking the other way. I walked around my home like a ghost, everything I touched seemed to fade into the air, all could see a mere reflection of me, but never me. Because I was tucked away somewhere behind the brave mask everyone kept pulling up every time it slipped.

I thought about what my aunt said about my mother having a good life. She did have a good life. But what did she teach me? I sank into the living room couch, thinking deeply about the woman for whom even the trees seemed to bow and shed leaves almost like a carpet with each step she took. I thought about my mother. I thought about that day in the park.

"No, no mommy, don't let me go." Six-year-old me screamed every time the swing went up, away from the ground. I remember thirteen-year-olds looking my way and laughing. Some laughed because they thought I was adorable, some were just teasing. When the swing slowed down and I could feel the ground under my pink boots, I looked at my mother who appeared blurry because of my teary eyes. I hugged her and made her promise to never push me on the swing again.

My mother bent down so that we were eye to eye, wiped the tears on my cheeks and asked me, "Are you sure you never want to play on the swing set again?" I looked at it and thought about it for a while.

"No. I like it."

"Then? Why do you cry?"

"Because I am scared I might fall."

"Sweetheart, but that is life. You are scared of the way, the journey. The way is always tough and uncertain. But, the end honey, the end makes it all worth it." My mother said, pulling me into a hug.

I didn't understand what she meant back then, but I do now. I remember I felt happy when I was at the top, when the swing took me the highest it could. The going up was what scared me. I was so certain I would fall, but every time I went up, I wanted to do it all over again.

"Sahana! Did you eat at all today?" My cousin's voice brings me back to reality. I sit up straight and look at her. I had been avoiding her too, cutting all the conversations short afraid she'd want me to get back to live again.

"Yes, I ate breakfast." I answer.

"And it's time for dinner now. Come along, let us eat."

I wanted to yell at her to stop trying. I wanted to tell her that I didn't feel hunger, I felt nothing but emptiness. I felt empty, needing my mother every day, longing for her. "I'm not hungry, Mer." I tell her. She sighed and sat beside me on the couch, took my hand in hers and whispered, "I know it's hard for you. It is hard for me too." I looked at her then, suddenly awakened by the thought that Mer, my cousin needed me too. Of course, she was hurt too. She just wanted to share her grief with me. "But it's been a month now, we have to go on with our lives. We cannot put our lives on pause now." I didn't want a pause button, I wanted the stop button. "I am not hungry, Mer." I take a last look at her broken face and get up to leave the room. I hear her sniffle, I hear her break down slowly, I hear her calling me for, but I do nothing. Instead, I think about the November morning with my mother and Mer.

"Mom, I don't think Mer is alright." I remember running downstairs to my mother who was baking in the kitchen.

"What happened to her?" she asked me, wiping her hands with the towel.

"She is crying. She said she doesn't want to ever talk to me."

"Why? Did you hurt her?"

"Yes mom, I lost her Barbie's left shoe."

"Oh no, not the shoes. Everyone needs a proper pair of shoes."

I looked at her apologetically and shrugged, "I never meant to do it on purpose."

She smiled at me and said, "Come with me, we can make this alright." She took the cookies out of the oven and placed them on a plate, the delicious smell wafted in the air.

We go upstairs to find Mer on the bed, tears streaming down her face. When she looked at me, I could smell the anger, "Go away, I don't want you here Sahana."

"Oh but she has something for you."

My mother motioned for me to move to her and give her the cookies as a peace offering. Mer stared at me for a long time, took the cookie and surprised me by breaking it into two and giving me the bigger piece. I ran to hug her and felt the world getting a little better. With Mer, it was easy, liking walking into a maze and already knowing your way out of it. My mother hovered around us and whispered in my ears, "There is nothing you can't ever fix. There is always a way-out honey, remember that."

Two months had gone by, and every morning that I woke up, I felt the loss as if it were yesterday. Maybe it was yesterday because I don't remember living any day since my mother's death. Mer wanted me to live again, it was hard to live when everything that made you feel alive was sucked out of you.

I decided going to school was all the living I needed to do. A sea of stares engulfed me, drowned me with concern. Suddenly everyone wanted to know where I was at all times, they were scared I might do something to harm myself, what they didn't know was that all harm had already been done.

"Can I have lunch with you?" My best friend stood with her tray at the end of the lunch table.

"Of course." I pat at the seat beside mine.

"How are you holding up, Sahana?"

"I'm better." I take a bite of my salad and say.

"You're eating just tomatoes for lunch?"

"Yeah, I happen to like tomatoes."

"C'mon you know what I mean." I giggle but say nothing.

"I have been worried about you, you don't talk to me anymore." She confesses.

"I know Sara, I do. I've been fine."

"You don't look fine, when was the last time you had a face mask on?" she jokes, poking me with her spoon.

"I look what I feel." I say and stare at my plate, it was a bad call with the tomatoes.

"Can I come over after school today?" Sara asks me, pushing a generous amount of rice on my plate. I smile at her. I don't know if I want to talk to anyone, as if I lost all the words between wanting to say them and wondering how to say them.

"Sara is a good friend, Sahana. Don't ever let her go. Even if she does, give her a reason, ten reasons to come back." My mother's voice danced in my head as I heard myself agreeing for our little meet.

Sara comes home just after an hour after our school was done. She had come before in the past few weeks, each time she was sent away before she could come in.

"So this is where you hide." She remarks as she enters my room, seeing books of poetry sprawled across the floor.

"Yes, you found me." I smile and pick up the book closest to my foot.

"Did I really find you?" Sara sits on the bed and watches me struggle put on the mask I had in front of the world.

"What do you mean?" I ask, knowing exactly what she meant.

"You know what I mean, you have been lost since forever. I am tired of looking now, please let me help you." She tells me sincerely.

"I don't know, Sara. I don't want to be found."

"Oh, hush. Let's catch up." She rubs her hands together and winks at me. I join her on my bed and sigh, "Let's."

Sara smiles at my response and fills me in with the latest gossip, until all I can think of is how much I've missed since the last few weeks. She was the touch of reality I needed.

In between laughing and getting amused, I felt a sudden pain in my heart, my mother still won't come back. She had gone on trips before, but she came back, with the gifts even. But this time, it was for real. She boarded her last flight and will never come back and wave at me as I stay waiting at the Arrivals section of the airport. I zone out thinking about my mother once again.

"Here, you forgot your lotion." I hand my mother her favourite scented lotion.

"What would I do without you?" she takes it from me and smiles.

"How long will you be going for now?" I sit cross legged on the bed, her clothes carelessly spread on her bed.

"A week, honey. Quick, tell me, which one, the blue or the black?" she asks me, holding up two scarves.

"The blue, you look good in blue." I say and watch her shift personalities between my mother and a woman chasing dreams until they knocked at her door.

"Why do you have to go away all the time?" I ask her, finally stopping her.

"Never. I will always come back. I won't leave you, my sweet."

She pulled me in a hug.

"Even if I do, you know where to find me."

"And where will that be?" I ask her.

"You know." She winks at me and gets back to packing.

After walking Sara out the door, I put on my jacket. And for the first time since months, I felt excited. It was as if I was going on an adventure with myself. I was excited, each step I took I felt the sadness falling behind me, failing to catch up with me. I could feel it slip off me like it was tired of me or maybe I was tired of carrying it on my back.

I run as if I am desperate to get back every day I lost believing my life was over. I run and smile because I know where to find her, I know where my mother is. I run as if that's all I know. I run because on the other side, there's me waiting for me. I run to the park where my mother and I come every time we just can't keep up with the world.

I am glad to see there's no one there. I speed to the closest bench I see and sit there, feeling the roses enchant me with their scent and cast a spell on me. I am taken back to when my mother and I came here when I got my heart broken for the first time.

"It is so peaceful here." I inhale the scent of the jasmine, teleporting me to another universe.

"It is." My mother agreed.

"Mom, I don't feel well. It hurts so badly." I lay my head on her shoulder.

"I know, sweetheart. Sometimes, it hurts to exist, all you want to do is hide in blankets and sleep for days. But you have to wake up, you have to get up. You have to keep going when your heart and soul have been shattered and shoved away. You cannot put your life on hold because it will be over before you know. You have to live and experience and grow. Please, for me, don't ever stop. Don't stop believing in the magic of tomorrow, anything could happen tomorrow,

all you have to do is be able to get through today. Promise me, you will keep going."

I didn't know how or when I started crying, but I felt relieved, as if someone had whispered the best thing in my ear and I just knew I would be fine. I get up to leave. On my way home, I walked feeling myself more and more each second. It felt as if I had reconnected with my long-lost friend. For the first time in ages, I smiled at people I knew rather than turning and taking a new dreaded way home.

My aunt was right. My mother taught me a lot, every day she told me a little more about life. I take out the brave mask I've been wearing, I didn't need to anymore. I am brave.

I make my way to my room to find Mer on my bed reading one of my books. She looks up at me, almost expecting me to ask her to leave the room. I give her my best smile, "Do you know what happened?" She pats on the bed enthusiastically, yelling yes in four different languages. No amount of darkness could beat the light in her eyes. And just like once again, all was starting to feel right with the world.

3

BHOPAL TO BANGLORE [B2B]

by Raghavi Shankara Guhan

On a hot and humid afternoon, an extremely tired Akshara entered the Bhopal Railway station dragging her small, ready to explode black suitcase behind her. It was very small and not enough to stuff the volumes of reference books she had brought along to aid in her research. Her clothes were so little that they would even fit her handbag, but her heavy books made her life difficult, especially in a humid and sweaty climate.

She glanced at her watch to check the time, it was exactly 3.00pm, she smiled to herself, she had ample amount of time before her train arrived at 5.00pm. Exhausted from her long bus journey from Indore to Bhopal, she sat down with a thud in a vacant seat which she found on the designated platform where her train was going to arrive, and within seconds her eyes drooped to let her drown in the world of sleep, as her weariness got the better of her.

An ear-piercing horn shook Akshara awake from her dreamland only to make her realize that she dozed off while waiting for her train. Immediately her eyes drifted to her wristwatch, to realize that it was 5.05pm and her train could depart any minute. Akshara reached out to her tiny black suitcase as she walked towards the train waiting on the platform - as she searched for her name in the reservation list, she was stupefied as her name seemed to be invisible in the list.

She rechecked the list a few times as her blood pressure continued to rise, finally, after making sure that magically, her reserved tickets were not seen on the list, she decided to make sure if she was looking at the right train, that is where another detail caught her attention making the ground slip beneath her feet. The list she was looking at belonged to some unknown train and not the one she had got tickets for; It was not the Grand Trunk Express but instead of some other train!

She was thunderstruck! As her brain ran through all the possibilities, her heart was sinking more and more, it was important for her to get back to Indian Institute of Science (IISc) in time to continue her research and here it appeared that destiny had different plans.

Pulling herself together, she decided to approach the railway inquiry person to get details of her invisible train, she was beyond confused as to how the train which was supposed to have arrived by now is not here yet: "Has it already left the station?? Or delayed??" with all these million thoughts running in her head, she quickly walked towards the help desk.

Upon reaching she pulled out the ticket from her handbag. As she forwarded it, she asked the questions that had been running in her head: "Uncle, how come the train which was supposed to arrive by 5.00 is not here yet, it is already going to be 5.15, is it delayed??". The aged man with rimmed glasses reached out to the ticket held in Akshara's hand and took a good look at the ticket. A smile crept on his face, he casually replied "Madam, the train arrived and also left on time". A confused Akshara proceeded to argue "How can it be sir, I have sat here since 3 in the afternoon, the train didn't even come, and you are saying it left!!" The old man replied: "Oh, madam, the train came at 5am and left at 5.20am, the ticket says 05.00 not 17.00" saying so he left the desk to grab a cup of tea with his colleagues in the office room.

Akshara was left speechless as she didn't know how she could commit such a blunder. She was guilty as to how based on her own calculations for the time the train would take to travel from Bhopal to Delhi and back, she had confirmed that surely her train was going to be in the evening without paying a second glance to double-check her assumption.

Due to the shock she received, she was rooted to her spot for quite some time, such that the person who spoke to her earlier had already returned to his spot after a brief tea-break with his friends. Seeing Akshara looking lost, he called out to her "Madam! You are still here? Next time when you book tickets, do check it. There is a decent hotel nearby, maybe you can rent a room and stay overnight in Bhopal. Be sure to get your tickets for tomorrow's train. Such things happen often madam, don't worry."

Hearing his words, drops of tears started to stream down from Akshara's eyes. How she wished it were as simple as it sounded, she hardly had any money with her. The accommodation she got in Indore, in a guest-house adjacent to the research facility was for free. Her guide from IISc had spoken to his contacts in the facility to allow Akshara to use the instruments she needed for her research, but other than that she hardly owned any money to be able to afford a room for a stay in Bhopal. Furthermore, she was a female at the prime of her adulthood and at that point (1990's), a lone lady was always thought to be a treat to the eyes of men. She felt utterly miserable and threatened as every eye set on her made her shrink inward more and more, as she felt like a prey being surrounded by hunters.

Looking at this state of Akshara, the inquiry-man felt sympathetic towards the young lady, possibly because he also had a daughter of her age and could understand her fears of staying alone, overnight in an unknown city.

He spoke "Madam, don't worry, where do you need to go? If you tell me, I will see if I can help you in any way, do not cry!". Hearing him, a spark of hope took birth in her small almond eyes. She quickly wiped away her tears before replying: "Actually, my final destination is Bangalore uncle, the Grand Trunk Express was supposed to take me to Chennai from where I would catch a bus to Bangalore."

Listening to her a smile broke on the face of the elder man, "Seems like it is your lucky day madam, there is a special train today running from Delhi to Bangalore, and fortunately most of its compartments are unreserved except a few, you can buy tickets for the unreserved compartment and go directly to Bangalore!"

Akshara couldn't describe the happiness she felt upon hearing about this special train. However, she was still skeptical about travelling in an unreserved compartment as it would mean anybody could come and go inside those compartments compromising her safety. So, she decided to keep mum while planning within her head on how to proceed.

After thinking through she asked the man: "I will grab my tickets from the ticket counter, but would you be kind enough to tell me which platform and time the train would arrive as I would proceed to the respective platform to wait. The man smiled again "It's your luck again, madam, the train standing right behind you is the very train I was talking about, it leaves in another 20 minutes, so you have ample time to get your tickets."

She was overjoyed with the knowledge that the train she had assumed to be the grand trunk express was in fact the special train that was going to carry her directly to Bangalore. She quickly checked the amount of cash she had and after putting aside some she proceeded to buy her ticket using the remaining she held in her hand.

After a relatively short queue of 2 people, she was out with her unreserved compartment ticket, and with 10 minutes to spare for the train to depart.

Checking the watch to confirm the time she proceeded to board the train, but instead of the unreserved compartment, whose ticket she had, she boarded the reserved compartment as she had planned.

Yes, she had put aside a sum of money to pay to the ticket collecting officer as a fine because she was going to climb the reserved compartment even with a ticket for the unreserved. To her, her safety was most important and deciding thus she had made up her mind to follow her instinct.

After climbing the reserved compartment, with a search of 10 minutes she found a seat near a family that was unoccupied and seated herself there. Just as she sat, the train jerked from its position and had slowly started to gain pace. She peered afar through the window as she saw the station where she thought she was stranded pass away in a blur as the train now completely moved out of it, into lush greenery. The surroundings entertained her with a beautiful scenic view, keeping Akshara staring, until she heard a girl around her age tap on her shoulder.

The girl was a part of the family, she concluded as all the other family members had their eyes upon the pair (the girl and Akshara). The girl spoke: "Hi! I am Namita, I noticed you looked a bit lost so thought I will give you some company! Hope you don't mind, my stupid brother has annoyed me so much that now I need some means of escape from his good-for nothing jokes."

Akshara smiled, this girl, Namita seemed to be sweet yet bold, she replied: "Hi Namita I am Akshara. I am very sorry for zoning out, I didn't notice you taking the seat beside me. I have had an almost nightmare-like day! Anyway, thank you for offering your company, it is so very sweet of you. Not many would do that!"

Namita smiled "Nice to meet you too!! You have such a beautiful name. Meet my family!" she said, pointing to her family sitting around them. Namita started introducing her seemingly never-ending family to Akshara, one by one, as Akshara smiled feeling overwhelmed at every introduction. Excluding Namita, the family had Namita's parents, her paternal uncle and aunt, her college going brother, and two school going twin cousins. This reaction of Akshara was maybe because this was the first time she was being introduced to a joint family. She had lost her father when she was in college and seeing such a beautiful joint family made her childhood memories with her small family return.

During the introduction, the father of Namita, Mr. Singh noticed Akshara tearing up and immediately got worried. He spoke "People! Wait see we are scaring the child, oh dear, why are you crying, did you hurt yourself?" He asked with concern evident as he placed a hand over Akshara's head checking her for any sign of injury as the other family members also joined and started questioning her endlessly for the reason for her tears. Meanwhile, looking at their reaction, Akshara was giggling because the family she just met seconds ago was giving her that kind of reaction that her family would probably give if they had been around.

She finally replied "Shhh! Oh gracious, how many questions, uncle, aunty and all the rest, I am not hurt in any way. In fact, it's the contrary, uncle had reminded me of my late father which made me tear up. I am completely alright!" All the while smiling as she brushed away the teardrops. The aunty replied: "Do not cry child, we are like your parents only, and consider this your family, be it just for a while, I am really happy to have met you!"

Akshara replied, "The pleasure is mine aunty, due to a huge blunder I thought I would be stranded on the streets of Bhopal, with hardly any money. But God's grace I got tickets for the unreserved compartments on this train which would take me directly to my destination. I am sorry I entered without tickets disturbed you in the reserved compartment."

Namita's aunt exclaimed: "Oh dear, I totally understand your concern, unreserved compartments are not at all safe, especially for pretty young ladies like yourself! And why do you say sorry! We are all very delighted to have met you!"

"Yes didi do not say sorry," said an 8-year-old Neetu, Namita's cousin and was immediately followed by her twin, Reetu who repeated the same; "Yes, no sorry!"

Seeing these cute munchkins, Akshara smiled forgetting all her worries. It was unbelievable as to how a family she met minutes ago seemed very homelike.

How blessed was she to have found a family in a place as unexpected as in a train compartment where she was not even supposed to be in. She recollected her day, and thought to herself, how lucky was she to have missed a train but having found a family in return!

As she was recollecting the day's happenings, she remembered something her father had once told her as a child, something that made sense to her now. He had said to little Akshara, "God never does anything without a reason. In every action of his, no matter how cruel it might seem, there is always a greater good hidden beneath those few moments of hardship. Boons are not always direct dear, sometimes they can be disguised as a curse too…"

Thinking about those childhood memories, she fell asleep, and the family left her to rest understanding that she had had a tough day.

As she slept, the family was busy making plans on feeding her the nutritious and scrumptious homemade delicacies they had packed for dinner.

4

THE FOREST OF SOULS

by Aashreya R

The day dimmed into darkness in the human realm. It was time to set another soul free. Nicholas looked back at the woods behind him. The Crystal wood forest. This was the place old souls who had completed all their responsibilities in the mortal world and died peacefully in their sleep, came after their demise. Here these souls, who had righteously fulfilled their purpose of life, spend the rest of eternity, in harmony, praying for others in the human realm, for their safety and salvation. The fog that separated the mortal world and the Crystal wood forest is called Phoenix Valley and it was Nicholas's job to guide new souls from the human realm into the forest. Nicholas couldn't help but wonder that in recent times the number of souls coming into the Crystal wood forest was getting lesser and lesser. Alas! Most humans in these times die before they truly realized themselves and their true purpose. After months of no work, one misty evening, his locket glowed golden, indicating the arrival of a new soul, at the entrance of phoenix valley. Nicholas sat upright, grabbed his silver staff, and walked briskly into the fog. There was a job to be done.

***

The grass felt cool against Jinora's feet. She opened her eyes and found lilac fog surrounding her. She felt lighter than usual. Almost pale. A minute later, frantically, she examined her hands. No scars. Jinora felt dizzy, confusion taking over her. That's when it struck her. She was dead and now a soul. Was this the afterlife? Is it still okay to be afraid of ghosts now that she was one too? Her mind was racing when she felt a hand on her arm. Jinora dodged and screamed.

"Who's that?"

From the lilac mist emerged a boy. He looked young, but his brown eyes gleamed wisdom, making him look like a relic, an ancient warrior. He smiled when he saw her, as if he was expecting to find her here.

"There is no need to fear me. I am Nicholas Adams. Keeper of souls at Crystal Wood forest and I am here to guide you, so that you may now rest in peace."

Jinora wondered if she was really dead or just having a really absurd dream. The boy who called himself Nicholas asked Jinora to hold his staff tightly and walk with him into the fog. Still dazed by what was happening, she obeyed. She couldn't help but notice the shining locket hanging across his heart. This is definitely a dream, she thought. Amidst everything a tiny thought was buzzing through her mind, the inevitable question.

If this place is where the dead go, would her Eleanor be here too?

***

Strange, Nicholas thought. Never before did a soul so young enter the forest. Not only was she young, but aggressive too, looking at everything around her wildly. He was used to the calm demeanour of old souls who would smile and take his staff as if they were expecting it. They had an aura of contentment around them.

The new soul was anything but calm. She was turbulent. Instead of warmth, he sensed a deep sadness in her aura. He couldn't believe someone as young as her had fulfilled her purpose in life and was onto eternal rest in the crystal wood. He couldn't help but feel awe.

"So tell me, how was the other side?" Nicholas asked

"I don't want to talk about myself."

Queer, thought Nicholas. Everything about the new soul felt out of place. All the souls he had guided through the phoenix valley had been more than happy to tell him their story. And there was more. In her eyes, he saw something he hadn't seen in a long, long time. Curiosity. The yearning for more.

Who was this girl?

He tightened his grip on the staff and walked faster.

Something was definitely wrong.

***

After an hour of walking silently Jinora felt the fog clear up. The sweet smell of leaves and the crisp cool air rushed through her. Ironic as it seemed, Jinora felt alive.

In front of her, she found a lush green endless terrain of trees. They were at a higher ground, she realized. Lakes flowing, the spread of moist grass, birds chirping, she almost felt like she was in heaven. Well… technically she was in heaven. She let go of the staff.

Nicholas noticed a tattoo on her arm that said 'per aspera ad astra'.

Through dust, to stars.

"I've always found Latin to be fascinating," he said.

"You are aware about the languages in our world?" Jinora asked

"I know a great deal more than the languages. Your world was once mine too."

Jinora looked at him, mildly surprised. "How did you end up here then?"

Nicholas smiled. Finally, someone asked him his story.

"It was a long time ago when I was in the mortal world. I lost both my parents in a fire accident. We had no extended family and being shy, I had no friends. My parents were my entire world and when I lost them, I was shattered, I had nothing to do and nowhere to go. I spent days sitting by my parent's grave holding my mother's chain in my hand, crying. And when I had no tears left, numbness took over. I had no purpose. Many nights passed until one moonless night, I saw a stream of light flowing towards me. A few seconds later the stream rose up and formed into a woman. She looked godly, angelic and I thought the angels had come to rescue me. But then she said she was the angel of death. Never did I think that death would look this beautiful. I told her my despair, and my lack of purpose. She took my mother's chain from my hand and whispered something into it. The locket glowed."

Then she said, "I will give you a purpose, for I have seen you sit determinedly at your loved one's grave. You will be the keeper of souls, guardian of those who rest. Guide the souls to their peace and find yours in them."

He turned toward Jinora looking at her in the eye.

"And that is how I ended up here, dear new soul. Because I refused to let my grief consume me and because the death had a heart"

***

Jinora felt compelled by the boy's story. She wanted to know more. But she didn't pry into it, she wanted to find Eleanor as soon as possible and maybe now they would be together, forever. The forest Jinora was walking into was more beautiful than anything she had ever seen, the vines seemed like they had fairy lights on them. When she looked closer, she saw that they were actually a ton of fireflies sitting on them. Nicholas told her that it was always evening in the forest. The weather was always pleasant and cool. They walked through different caves with different souls, resting. Nicholas was narrating to her the stories of their lives.

They passed through a fountain and by its side, they found an old woman with a tranquil face. She smiled at them softly. Nicholas nodded at her and said, "She is Marsha. She lived humbly and dedicated her entire existence to feed the poor. She may have approximately fed a million people during her life in the mortal world. She fulfilled her purpose and now she rests in peace."

After passing through a pond, they arrived at a rose garden. The tender smell of red roses stopped Jinora, between the roses sat another woman. Her eyes were closed. Her face radiated divinity. The kind of face poets would die to write poetry about.

Jinora asked Nicholas about her and he said, "She is Evelyn. The greatest female artist of her age. Her art was wild and immortal and transcended time. She paved the way for self-expression and evolution for centuries that followed."

They moved on. As they explored the forest, Jinora's fascination grew. Waters filled with stardust, fruits which looked like jewels, flying gypsies teasing them, all amidst the wintry sublime backdrop of eventide. Jinora met many other souls and heard their tales. But she was getting anxious. Everyone here was old. She wondered if the forest was categorized by age and perhaps, they were just passing through the elderly side of it. However, minutes later they reached a great canyon with a circular inscription on it. Nicholas turned to her and said "This is it. This is the end of our forest. Once I place my locket on the inscription, your soul will be secured here forever."

Jinora began to panic. The end?

She moved ahead of him and asked, "This might sound weird, but did a girl of my age named Eleanor come here too, a few days ago?"

Nicholas looked perplexed and said, "Another young girl? I'm afraid not. You are the first of your age to enter the crystal wood forest."

Jinora's mind was spiralling, "First of my age? What are you talking about?"

"This enchanted forest is the home for souls who have left their mortal bodies after the fulfillment of all their duties in the human realm."

"But I think there is a mistake, I have done nothing. I shouldn't be here," said Jinora growing impatient by the minute

"Trust the judgement of death, dear soul."

With that Nicholas moved to the canyon. Jinora paced towards him and pushed him

"I haven't done anything. In fact, I've done the worst of things."

Nicholas looked at her and saw that her eyes glittered with tears. "I killed myself, Nicholas Adams, I killed myself."

***

"You killed yourself?" said Nicholas as if these words were alien to him.

"I didn't want to," Jinora replied. She talked rapidly now, as If she was running out of time. "I was miserable. I was having a panic attack. You don't know our world Nicholas, it's cruel! I just wanted a physical let out. So, I cut myself. I guess it went too deep. The next thing I know I'm here."

"Why were you miserable?" he asked.

Jinora put her face in her hands. She did not want to think about it. Eleanor's pale face, their broken dreams.

"Talk to me," Nicholas said

'This is crazy. I am stuck in the afterlife, with a spirit guide therapist' thought Jinora as she began to tell Nicholas her story.

"I lost my best friend six days ago. We have been friends since we were one. We loved the same things and had the same aspirations. We even had a podcast together. We were working on so many wonderful things together and then boom! One day, I showed up at her home, looking at her in a casket. Everything blurred in that moment. The bicycle rides we took when we were young, the double brownie ice cream we used to make, the calls which turned into ted talks when one of us felt low, our clenched hands, every single aspect of our friendship came back rushing into me in that moment. It was too much. I ran back to my home and locked myself in my room. They say grief reduces with time, but every moment catalysed my misery. I couldn't do anything. I felt… cursed.

"Every curse is a blessing in disguise." Nicholas told, as Jinora looked at him, her eyes red now "My mom used to say that to me all the time. I understand your pain new soul, I do. Losing your loved ones is the greatest of sorrows. But I want to tell you something. Suffering is inevitable, misfortunes and problems are never going to stop coming. However, let me remind you, they are what makes the end worth it. Marsha? The lady at the fountain? She was abandoned by her family, but she didn't let that be her story. She sometimes jokes with me that she is grateful that her family left her. She was able to find a better family who are kind and care about the world. Evelyn was an outcast. She was publicly shamed in her town. People threw rocks at her for being the imaginative genius she was and for being a woman. Years passed Evelyn used all of her grief to fuel her and filled her paintings with trauma and hope. The same town now has a museum dedicated to her. The nights are always long and dark. But every dark night will come to an end, the sun will come out again and then it's the time to shine.

Jinora was taking in all his words when Nicholas walked to her and placed his locket on her arm above her tattoo. It burned her. She tried to resist, but then she saw the light spiralling around them swiftly, like a whirlpool. Nicholas came closer, smiled, and whispered into her ear. Then he moved outside the spiral and asked, "What is your name?"

"Jinora"

"It was nice meeting you Jinora. I will await your return."

Jinora wanted to say it back, but the spiral wound around her completely, light blinded her, and the darkness took over.

***

Jinora woke up with a start.

Was that all a dream?

She rushed to the mirror and looked at her arm.

Per aspera ad *astra*

And above that was a thin circle.

It was real. She had been given a second chance. To live, to serve.

Outside, the dawn broke. The first rays of sunshine entered through the window onto Jinora's face. Nicholas's last words, the ones he whispered, were still reverberating in her brain.

"Bright is the light that comes after the eclipse. Go back. Go back and Find out what you're made of, finish the wars you left unfinished. Learn what every obstacle is trying to teach you. Every time it feels like the end, begin again. And then when all is done, drift back here, to peace, to me. The forest and the valley, and I will wait for you dearly."

Jinora looked back into the mirror.

"I will."

She opened the door, stepped out of her bedroom.

She was going to make Eleanor proud.

She was going to begin again.

5

DANCE OFF

by Aashritha Kadiri

There I was on the stage, dancing my heart out and then suddenly I heard a snap, and then I fell to the ground, in pain. The song stops. 5 minutes after I am on the ground, I hear people coming to help me, those five minutes felt like 5 hours, it was like no one could see me.

There I was on the ground in pain that can't be explained, and the audience did nothing, just sat there and I could hear them whisper in shock, but I don't blame them, they couldn't do anything, they just couldn't rush up the stage, but I expected one of the 2 people who I thought were my friends to come. I expected them to come and pick me up and then help me, but they didn't. They weren't even looking, well they kind of were but not with concern, they were recording me. I was suffering, and what they were doing, they were on their phones.

My life was spinning out of control, I am not just talking about this dance, the past year was, let's just say crazy. A few months ago, I started going to Granite High School. We had to move schools as we were moving houses, and my old school was too far away. So new house, new school.

When I first moved to Granite High, I was pretty sad, I mean all my friends were at my previous school and I was the best dancer there, I was popular, had good grades. I had everything, and when I moved to Granite High I lost it, I lost it all, except for the dance part. I was pretty good, maybe even better than some of the others, well at least until I hurt myself.

Once I came, it was pretty clear that Mia and Oliva were the popular ones, they were the center of attention, everyone wanted to be them. And If I am being honest, so did I, I wanted to become popular again.

So well, I did what every person who would wanna be popular would do, went up and spoke to them. I think it is safe to say that it didn't go well, they aren't me to go bug someone else, but that wasn't gonna stop me from getting what I want.

Well, you see I am so determined and competitive, so no matter what, I always get what I want. I noticed that they wear black jeans with a pink crop top. And I had the exact same ones, well not exact, but close enough, but I don't like to wear them. With their posture, it was easy to tell that they were cheerleaders, and I am a dancer, but they were also mean and put on a lot of makeup and I want that, if I'd do that I would be changing myself. From my dress to my attitude, if anyone from my old school would see me, they wouldn't even know who I am.

If I knew that time when I met these girls, that this wouldn't end well for me. I would not have done this, and I wouldn't have tried to change who I was just to be part of the popular group, but I guess you can't change the past.

At that moment, I decided that I am getting on the girl group, no matter what.

Right then, I found out something that could maybe help me get on the group, there were cheerleader tryouts the next day. Pretty early in the year for cheer though, but that wasn't going to stop me. I went home that day and then worked on my routine that I would use for the tryouts.

Then the next day, I wore the black jeans and a pink crop top and went to school, and to my surprise they actually complimented me. Once I passed them in the hallway, they said "What was your name again?" "Anglica", I replied.

"Nice outfit Anglica, you dance?" Mia asked .

"Yeah, how'd you know?"

"You have the cheerleader tryouts poster in your hand"

"Right."

So far so good, I thought to myself

"Okay then, see you after school" Mia and Oliva said at the exact same time. It was like they are robots or something.

I had math last period right after, I went to the auditorium for the tryouts, I wasn't nervous or anything but instead, I was kinda excited. The last time I was nervous, I ended up ruining the whole dance audition, so since then, I would tell myself that I am getting in or winning no matter what. That is also why I am so determined to get what I want.

Lucky for me, I nailed my audition, Oliva and Mia were really impressed and I got on to the team! After the audition, Oliva and Mia came up to me and said:

"Great audition, Anglica."

"Yea, thanks I am really excited to be-"

"Yeah yeah, now to the important stuff" Oliva interrupted

"Um, important stuff?" I replied

"Yea, we always have a group of 3, it used to be me, Oliva, and Rachel" "But then Rachel left the school for some other school, and it was only me and Mia. We want you to be one of us! Great right!"

Bingo! I thought to myself "OMG really- and then I was interrupted again this time but Oliva.

"Yea blah blah, now listen up, if you are going to be one of us, you need a makeover."

"Like as soon as possible."

After that very absurd conversation, Mia and Oliva took me to the washroom, and then you can bet that they changed me completely even more that I would change myself.

Now I hear you saying it, "There is no way they can change you so much and even if they did, you could easily just say no and then walk out," And yeah, maybe you are right dear reader, but I have heard from many people that Mia and Oliva spread rumours like that, and people actually believe them. So no, if I want to finish school here I need to have a good reputation, so I just decided to go with it.

They started off by saying that my outfit was fine and will have to wear it back and pink every single day. Honestly, I didn't really like pink or black, so well, I was doomed already. Then they said that I had to always put my hair completely down or half up and half down. I really didn't like that, I preferred putting my hair up in a high ponytail, guess I am not doing that anymore. Then they told me about my makeup, which may not sound that bad until they said I could only put shades of pink or red. Did I mention I don't like pink? Then finally a thing that I might like, I need to be on the cheer team, have been there, done that, and participate in the huge dance competition thing in 3 months. I am actually excited about that, at least I was at that time.

After the whole thing I asked them when will they start the whole makeover thing, they laughed and said "Gurl, by makeover we meant just to tell you about it not actually do your makeup and all, just do it on your own in your time, we haven't got time to prepare you and the reason we are in the washroom is that this is a secret and this washroom is only for the cheerleaders and since all the other cheerleaders left, we have this place all to ourselves."

"Um okay!" I was more than confused, who says it is a makeover and then doesn't give them a makeover, not that I wanted one anyway. After all that, I could finally go home. Once I reached home, I finished my homework, had dinner and I went straight to bed.

The next day I wore a black skirt with a pink off-shoulder top, put my hair half up and did my make up and went down for breakfast. Mum was shocked, she asked me if I was in a play and was doing this for that. A play? I am a dancer, not an actor!

I laughed and said, I was part of the popular girls now. Mum looked at me and asked, "Anglica, don't you think you are changing yourself for others?"

"No, I am just wearing different closets and I am wearing a different hairstyle and I am wearing makeup! Ugh.. okay, just because I am looking a little different doesn't mean I am changing myself, okay mum?"

"Whatever you say sweetie, but remember you are perfect the way you are"

"I know"

After that, I went to school and for some reason, Mia and Oliva were standing in front of the school. Maybe it was like something they always do! I thought to myself, well, I was wrong, they wanted to see if I was "dressed correctly" and they had to make sure I was dressed like a "popular girl" and to my surprise, they told me that I nailed my outfit, it was weird.

While we were going in, a guy tripped and his books went everywhere, I started to walk towards him so that I can help him, but Mia and Oliva stopped me, then they said, "You a popular girl now Angelica and rule number one- never talk to the nerds!"

I am not going to lie. I felt bad for him, and I was mad at Mia and Oliva. So mad that I said, "What is wrong with you two, we should go and help him!" Once I said that I started walking towards him but then I stopped, I heard Mia talking to Oliva about me.

"OMG Oliva, what do you think everyone will say if we tell them that Anglica had to leave her other school because she bullied a kid there."

I spun around, then I looked back, the guy was looking at me, I turned back and whispered sorry and walked towards Mia and Oliva.

"No more talking to the 'Nerds' let's go now."

It was killing me not helping people, but I couldn't risk my reputation, could I?

Fast forward to 2 months, 3 weeks, and 3 days, the past few months were pretty much the same, they would try and control every single thing I do, they changed me completely. I couldn't admit it or confront them. I don't really know why. I started working on the dance for the dance competition 2 months back and so far it is going good. It was a ballet dance. I love ballet so much and its elegance and the emotion you need. I just love it, so I thought why not just do this for the competition.

And that is also the first thing Mia and Oliva liked that I also liked. Mia and Olivia were also competing in the competition, they were doing a duet. When I asked why we all couldn't do a trio they said that I wasn't skilled enough to compete with them. I wasn't skilled enough?! Now I may be a little overconfident, but I am more than sure that I am way better than both of them combined!

I had a plan from then on to go onto that competition and crush Mia and Olivia. They were going to go down!

And well that was the plan until the day of the competition, it was like every single thing was going wrong. The day started off bad and just went worse.

It started off with me missing my alarm, then me forgetting my pointe shoes so I had to run back home halfway then I tripped and fell, I kinda twisted my ankle maybe I wasn't really sure, but I ignored it and ran home and got my shoes and ran back to school. I was lucky my home is within walking distance. Once I got my pointe shoes, I ran up to my class.. I was late and we had a surprise test. I am the kind of person who believes that if a day starts out bad it only gets worse and there is no way it can get better. It is negative I know, but that is the way I am. The rest of the school day was… let's just say horrible. The more the day went on, my ankle started to get worse, I decided to go to the nurse at lunch, as a dancer I know it isn't safe to dance with an injury and the nurse said it was nothing. I figured it was all in my head.

Then it was time to compete, thankfully nothing went wrong until I went on stage. I had to do pirouettes on pointe,

I don't know what happened, but I fell, I fell, and I heard a snap, I fell to the ground in pain and it was like I was imperceptible to others.

A few minutes later, the guy whom I didn't help, whose books were all over the place called the nurse, while Mia and Oliva were just standing there, recording me or just being on their phones, I knew they were selfish but never thought they would be this selfish.

Once the nurse came she took me to the hospital, turns out I fractured my ankle. Fast forward 6-10 weeks later, my ankle healed pretty well , but I can't dance right now or even walk without crutches. I don't know if it is that I am not ready or if it is all in my head, but this time I am going to wait until I feel okay. Me and that guy, whose name is Justin, we became good friends.

I confronted Mia and Oliva about why they didn't help me. You can make sure that I am no longer a part of that popular girls group, but that doesn't matter. Though this experience wasn't the most fun or appealing, it really showed me that I shouldn't change myself for anyone and that I am perfect the way I am. Well, maybe not perfect ,but I am happy with who I am. I learned that friends aren't the ones who change who you are but who support you no matter what. And most importantly, I learned to listen to myself.

Coming to Granite High, was like an unfortunate event with a positive outcome, a blessing in disguise, every bad luck comes with good luck right?. These past few months were hard, but I am glad it happened, because now I have a true friend, I am stronger than ever and if someone wants to change me, that ain't happening!

6

THE SOUL MATE

by Anoushka Sharma

When a person lives with the guilt, even death seems better.

Memories of a dream that will never be a reality. Letters that never reached its destination, words lost their meaning with time. It's there in the sky where our moments are shattered. It's here in the darkness where my thoughts are scattered.

Love is dying. Reality is lying, but here I am crying. Broken promises, crushed heart, and bleeding scars, but I am not done yet!

Our souls may be shattered but I'll live life as a poet...

These were the words written on the front page of a fourteen-year old's diary. The age in which she should have had the dreams to fly. To live! Here she was living in hell and burning with guilt daily. Diary had a lot of poems, lots of letters to her sister, who could not read them now. She was gone! It had those plans of the future that seemed bleak now. And you know what else was there?

The plans to cut or die!

Can you even imagine it? No right! But she was like that. She lost her childhood and grew up too soon. In the past three years she had gone through the darkest of times, with none by her side and so those monsters in her head gave her the company she required. The difference was that these were not her friends. They punished her daily for something she had not done. They screamed in her head, making it difficult to concentrate. They choked her. She used to sweat, and her hands used to tremble fervently, and she had absolutely no control over it, anymore. They controlled her and she was just a broken puppet!

That night again, she sunk down a little deeper into the bathtub, pushing her head under the red water. She held herself there for as long as she could stand before sitting up, gasping for breath. She sighed as she grabbed the sharpest thing close to her, this time, it was a razor. She pressed it against her skin and took a deep breath as she slipped it against the outside of her arm. She watched as the deep crimson blood came to the surface and she let loose the tears that she had been holding for such a long time. This became her nightly ritual.

When the night sets in, she used to shut herself down. She had no motivation for anything. She told her no one cared, even though she knew that some really did. She thought about all the negative things she could possibly think of. She gave herself all the pain thinking she deserved it. The past was not letting her go! The memories of the haunted day ate a piece of her soul daily... She could not forgive herself. Guilt wasn't letting her go. She woke up suddenly, again that dreadful event in her dreams. She was sweating like anything.

FLASHBACK (Sheena's POV)

Tears stung my eyes and cheeks as they flowed down my face. I could feel them burning the back of my throat in a hot, salty lump. Despite the number of times I wiped my eyes, the deluge refused to stop. I couldn't move... couldn't breathe. My brain tried to comprehend all that happened but could barely keep up. I could see people rushing towards the ambulance. My sister, my soulmate was dead.

Her body was taken out of the ambulance. Her haunting brown eyelids stood out on her pale face. The grim set of her mouth and expressionless features looked out of place on her radiant, smiling face. The girl who used to run here and there was lying still and all I could do was stand at a distance and watch my angel go away.

PRESENT

Looking back, she remembered a thick, disorienting fog descending on her, making it difficult to think or act. Tears came fast and easy then, with no warning whatsoever. She wondered how she was going to get through this because everything looked bleak and hopeless. She was alive, but her will to live went away with her sister. At the young age of fourteen, the future, which had seemed so bright and promising, was momentarily obliterated, and forever altered.

By learning first-hand about pain and death, she grew up overnight, losing a piece of her childhood. She thought it was her mistake that she could not save her sister from drowning. And now, she was drowning daily in the pool of guilt. She felt lost as she wandered around aimlessly, looking for the light at the end of the tunnel.

One of the days, she came across a thing she had abandoned long ago, and that single thing changed her entire life.

She saw herself in a mirror. She saw the scars around her neck, the marks on her hands, the ghostly dark circles under her eyes and a firm face without any expressions. The same face that used to dazzle with the laughter seemed dead. All of a sudden, she saw a girl in the mirror. She looked like her. Same eyes, same lips... yet everything seemed different.

The girl in the mirror was dancing, laughing, her eyes had millions of dreams and a shine. Her smile was so pious that it could make anybody's day.

She carefully looked at that girl and found out that it was she, herself, when she was 12. She couldn't believe her eyes. How could it be her? Is it even possible? As she was thinking, she saw the girl in the mirror stretching her hand towards her as if calling her. She got scared. She couldn't understand what was happening. The mirror girl just asked her to smile and disappeared. And at that very moment, she realized, *the girl in the mirror was an illusion.*

That day, she forced a smile. Stretched her lips thin and formed them into a smile. She smiled for the first time in years. And that smile changed the world for her. The positivity that was lost, came back again. She could feel something after so long. It provided her positive energy, it provided her hope. Hope to be happy. Hope to live. Hope that her sister will forgive her. Hope to fulfill her broken dreams.

Today, she was guilty too, but no longer about the thing she had no control over. Instead, she was guilty of making herself unhappy. She was guilty of building her walls too high. Guilty of being so mad at those who left, that she forgot to appreciate those that were there all along. Guilty of holding onto grudges. Guilty of trying so hard to plan her future (which she learnt, was not even guaranteed), that she forgot to focus on her present. Guilty of sometimes letting people get her down.

Guilty of not doing what she wanted, because of the constraint by society. Guilty of letting her emotions run her life. Guilty of succumbing to rejection and allowing herself to believe that she was a failure. She was guilty of not appreciating her parents, her friends. Guilty for not appreciating the education she got to receive. Not appreciating the plate of food on her table, served to her three times a day. Not fully appreciating the people when they were there. Not appreciating all the moments she called her 'good days', because she was holding onto her 'bad days'.

She was guilty for not believing in herself. Guilty of not saying enough, not laughing enough!

And now she had no desire to get even with any of them for how they dragged her down. For the past belonged to those hard times- they could keep it. But the future? It was hers!

She learnt that if somebody wants, they can find a million reasons to hate life and to be angry with the world, or if you want, you can find a way to love this life and smile. And that single reason when weighed with the million ones weighs more. And that is YOU! You have to be happy for yourself!

She learnt not to regret the past, but to value it as it taught her so many things. It made her stronger. Today she is an author, and she has published all those letters and has titled it "Shanaya: Still the soul mate."

It is also true that time mends painful wounds. While she will never forget the beautiful and bubbly girl who was her sister, time and her smile has served to ease some of the intense pain. Every day she sees herself in the mirror and smiles, in the hope that her smile will reach Shanaya.

Now, she can say she has been through the valley, with its shadows, hopelessness, and darkness, but on the other hand, there is light, there is hope!

"Let your dreams be bigger than your fears, your actions louder than your words and your faith stronger than your feelings."

7

SAFELY ARRANGED

by Archana Natarajan

Ah! How terrible can things get Sowmya! I hate getting hitched in a typical Tam-Brahm setting. In the era of dating apps we are still relying on matrimonial websites," Sharan said pulling his hair in exasperation.

"I understand Sharan, but the truth is that we ended up finding each other through this whole arranged marriage set up," Sowmya consoled him holding his hand.

"Whatever….. I am glad to have found you," saying this he pulled Sowmya close and wrapped his arms around her waist.

"We have at least escaped the normal by choosing to date undercover. I can't believe it is almost a year since I have known you."

[Pause]

"But at times I also feel I don't know you enough," Sowmya said innocently. Hearing this, Sharan tightened his grip around her waist.

"Will you join me and my friends for a trip to Pondicherry?" Sharan asked Sowmya in a whisper. His warm breath was sending tickles down her neckline. She was quiet for a long time.

"What are you thinking Sowmya? It is a great opportunity to know each other better. A trip could get us closer. I can also introduce you to my friend. They will be accompanied by their wives."

"Relax; I was just cooking up a reason for travelling to Pondicherry," Sowmya said, releasing his grip.

"I hope you haven't told anyone that we have met before Sharan." They stood facing each other with their eyes glistening with excitement.

"You can mask your true nature so well. I never thought you would be so liberal considering the kind of traditional family you are surrounded with, that too in a place like Chennai. Even the calling bell sound is so typically Tam-Brahm," Sharan said laughing out loud. She laughed along.

That night Sowmya was in a completely different mood. She was nervous as well as excited. Their marriage date had been fixed for two months from now because of Sharan's official tour to Germany.

A fortnight later, they met again in Pondicherry. They were a group of six. It hardly took time for Sowmya to mingle with the others. Sharan made sure she was comfortable around his friends. They explored around together and strolled for hours along the beach. It was definitely assuring for Sowmya to see Sharan being his normal self while he was with friends. For the amiable and friendly nature of Sowmya, becoming everyone's favourite was not a difficult task. Sharan was also feeling assured after introducing her to his friends. He could see his love marriage dream coming true in an arranged marriage set up. After watching the sunset at the beach they came back to the resort. While entering names at the registration desk Sharan hesitated a bit but managed to loop in Sowmya with another girl.

Everything was going smoothly but when the time came to retire to their respective rooms, Sowmya felt a little awkward. Sharan took her cold and nervous hand into his warm grip. The other couples escaped with their respective partners quickly, leaving them behind to be with each other. Although Sowmya was too excited to be able to spend time with Sharan, she was also worried about trusting him completely. Her doubts were interrupted by Sharan's voice, "What are you thinking about Sowmya? We are going to be married in just a month's time. Don't worry when I am there." Sowmya felt assured with the confident and composed tone in his voice. She admired this quality in him.

The moment Sowmya put her bag down in the room and turned to close the door behind her, she was mid-air. Sharan held her tightly in his arms. After a lot of struggle she was brought down. He embraced her tightly and placed a light peck on her cheek. Sowmya was feeling extremely shy despite the adrenaline rush. They sat for almost an hour sharing stories about their childhood, expressing their thoughts about each other, and discussing the wedding preparations. With the beautiful romantic ambience in the room and the loving company of each other, Sharan and Sowmya got completely carried away and surrendered themselves to each other. Sowmya slept a dreamy slumber that night after Sharan planted a soft kiss on her forehead, taking a vow to keep her happy forever.

The morning after was a quick wrap up. Sowmya left for the bus station after giving a see-you-soon hug to Sharan. From then on, her thoughts were clouded only by Sharan and the memories of the time they had spent the previous day. Sharan reached Hyderabad the same night. Both got busy in their work life amidst the wedding preparations. They managed to catch up on their day-to-day updates through messages and calls. Each day was getting better and better as they started getting to know each other. A week had flown by.

One fine evening Sowmya was sitting gloomily in the bedroom surrounded by her mother and her aunts. Their discussion was revolving around Sowmya's delayed menstrual cycle and whether she should be taking the pill to postpone her cycle. Their concern was not about her, but about the wedding rituals which could get messed up; thanks to all those baseless menstrual taboos. Sowmya's mind was rejecting everything that they said. She was only worried if the reason for the delay could be their adventurous stunt in Pondicherry. Her thoughts froze. She kept nodding to everything her relatives said. She was hardly in a mood to debate. An appointment was fixed for the weekend with their family gynaecologist. Sowmya got petrified. She couldn't tell her mom to postpone the doctor's visit. It would raise doubts. She was in a dilemma. The only person whom she could call was Sharan. He did not take her calls. She left a message on WhatsApp.

'Call me please.'

'URGENT'

'I missed my P this month. You did use protection that night, right? '

'There is a lot of confusion at home. I am too nervous.'

'Please call me.'

'I hope nothing could have gone wrong.'

'I hope your protection was intact.' (10:50 PM)

There wasn't any reply or call from Sharan. Sowmya had a sleepless night. She kept checking her phone every ten minutes. Her mind was full of negative thoughts. She did a lot of research on the internet and found out multiple reasons for the delay, but one reason pointing out directly at her cause, seemed to be a by-chance-failed-protection. She decided to get herself tested for pregnancy. She was feeling ashamed. Suddenly the world seemed to be a dangerous place to live in. Going to the pharmacy and buying a self-testing home pregnancy kit was too risky plus she did not have the courage to approach a pharmacy. Finally! Google maps helped her in finding a small diagnostic laboratory in a two-kilometre vicinity of her house. It was a small and a dingy center but seemed to have a regular inflow of patients. With a lot of hesitation she got the test billed. She checked her phone; there was still no reply from Sharan.

"I am getting a pregnancy test done." (10:02 AM)

Sowmya gave the sample and waited for the result. Her hands trembled as she held the urine container and left it on the tray for testing. There were many other women seated around her. Many among them had come to get the same test done. The atmosphere was nauseating. Sowmya started linking her symptoms with all the junk she had read up online. She started imagining her future and the situation at home. She was worried if this was going to show up during the gynaecology consultation. She doubted if Sharan was purposely ignoring her messages. Fortunately, technology helped in clearing her doubts. He hadn't seen his messages from the previous night. She was thinking if he could have done all this on purpose, just to make her feel low. Her doubts multiplied. "Could he have done it just like a one-night fling and later he could cancel the wedding?", she thought.

After a while, a nurse came and handed over a pink slip. Sowmya read and re-read the report in shock. She reconfirmed the report with the nurse. It was 'POSITIVE'.

She felt as if she had been handed over a pink slip in school or college. Negative thoughts clouded her mind. She went to the extent of thinking about an abortion.

'It is POSITIVE. :-(What do I do now?' (10:40 AM)

The five-minute walk from the center to her office seemed the longest. She gulped her tears and went to work gloomily. With no response from Sharan after two days, she feared all her doubts would come true. She was not her normal self. She walked back home looking at her phone continuously. Seeing Sowmya's gloomy face, her parents suspected something was not alright. Sowmya made up reasons and warded off all doubts, but she couldn't convince herself. She cursed herself that night for trusting him so quickly and crossing the line before marriage. All those rubbish stories she had seen, read and heard of, seemed to be coming true. She started considering herself as a victim of betrayal.

Her thumbs were aching after swiping continuously over the cell phone. She willed herself to not check her phone to see if he had replied. It had been about three days. She hated that she was constantly checking his 'last seen at' status and yes, he had logged in just five minutes ago. Yet she couldn't stop herself. This sinking feeling to find absolutely no communication from him was becoming unbearable, almost torturous.

And then, just as she sat down in her chair, her phone vibrated. With her heart thudding in her ear, she unlocked her phone and stared at the screen. Finally! It was his message.

But when she opened it and read it, she nearly stopped breathing. She didn't know if he was joking or not. What was this?

'Babe……' (12:00 AM)

'Chill…….'

'Nothing could have gone wrong from my side.'

'I am sure about the protection being intact, but are you sure about yourself?'

Sowmya: 'What do you mean? ' (12:25 AM)

'So, you are doubting me?'

Sharan: 'Just the way you did. :-)'

'Before you start blaming me further, let me clarify, my mobile was inside the gym locker whose key I had lost. I got the key only today.' (12:30 AM)

Sharan called her immediately. He was not in a mood to argue with her and he did not want to give room for misunderstandings. Sowmya spoke to him in a shaky tone while he remained calm. Their voices went up and down in pitch, most of them being Sowmya's sobs. This minor incident was a testing stage in their relationship. They blamed each other. Sowmya, being the more vulnerable one was the most affected. She slammed the phone down and went to sleep vowing to handle the situation all by herself. Sharan was worried. He sent her multiple messages, but she did not reply. He apologized for doubting her instead. Sowmya saw all his messages but refused to reply. Two days went by. Sowmya had only one more day before the gynaecologist consultation. Basically, she had one day left to cover up the sin and find a solution.

Sharan was on the verge of losing his calm without being able to talk to Sowmya. He assured Sowmya that he would be by her side and they could manage the situation very well, even if the report were confirmed positive. He suggested she strike a deal with the gynaecologist and tell her the truth, but Sowmya was not convinced.

Amidst all this confusion Sowmya decided to talk to her close friend who was working in a hospital. She was too embarrassed to discuss intimate facts with her. After listening to the entire story Sowmya's friend suggested she should come to her hospital where she would get the test repeated.

To Sowmya's happiness and shock the result was 'NEGATIVE'.

'How is it possible?' Sowmya said, holding her head in her hand. She was hysterical and was almost on the verge of crying when her friend calmed her down. She analysed the situation in detail and assured that the test results in their laboratory were fool proof. There could have been something wrong with the other laboratory's report. Sowmya had never thought about that. Only because of her friend was she able to get a second opinion on the test. Feeling relieved and confused, she left for home. On the way back she went to the same laboratory where she had got her test done the first time. She took both the reports and showed them to the Pathologist. The doctor had a look at the reports and discussed it with her staff in detail. After a lot of interrogation it was concluded that there had been a gross mistake from the laboratory's end. Sowmya's urine sample's label had been exchanged with some other patient's label who could be pregnant. Sowmya raised a hue and cry there, but the emotional damage had been done. She left for home after threatening to sue their lab.

She was waiting to talk to Sharan and share the happy news with him.

She rang the bell hurriedly. She was waiting to barge into the house and rush to her room. To her surprise it was Sharan who opened the door for her and welcomed her with a bouquet of flowers. She pinched herself hard to believe that it was him. They greeted each other with a smile. Sowmya's parents were extremely happy to see Sharan pay a surprise visit just to see Sowmya. He took Sowmya out on a date that evening.

Over dinner Sowmya cleared the air by describing to him about the incident. He seemed to be relieved. He kept holding her hand throughout and gave it a gentle squeeze.

"I am really sorry if I hurt you in any way with my terse words. I am not the type to leave you and run away. Please trust me. Come what may, I will always stick by your side. Even if the report had turned out to be positive I would have helped you in finding a solution. It is not about your life alone now; it is linked to mine too."

Tears rolled down Sowmya's eyes. They were tears of joy and relief. All the confusion and emotional drama of the past week had finally come to an end. She was ready to go to any doctor now.

"I should also be sorry for not being able to trust you completely. I think we shouldn't have crossed the line," saying this Sowmya got up from the chair and turned away from him.

Let it go Sowmya, just relax. Twenty more days to go before you are mine forever,' saying this Sharan wrapped her in his arms tightly.

***

All's well that ends well. Sharan and Sowmya got married soon and from then on, there wasn't going to be any scope for such situations. Sowmya's friend and her timely advice was indeed 'A BLESSING IN DISGUISE' for the couple.

8

ATHEIST

by Prajwal Shukla

19 years ago, I was exactly like you. Exactly the same, maybe even worse than some of you present here today, in fact that's when my drinking problem started. You see, my… my son… Vikram, he, uh.. he… was excellent at playing cricket, he was excellent, or as I correctly recall some of his peers and juniors would say, a legendary cricket player. He was simply excellent. I was a proud father. I've always been a huge fan of the game and well, so was he. He grew up seeing me watch cricket on the television, and sat with me watching it, and that's how his interest in the game began. I still remember when he showed interest in playing cricket in the street with his friends as a child, and I encouraged him to take this one step further, and so year, after year, after year, and he kept getting better at it, the more he practiced, the better he got. He won his school a trophy, and scored well on his report card, the parent-teacher meetings I attended were all praise and no complaints. He balanced his practice and his academics right. All his teachers were happy, and our family was honoured in the community when he won himself a silver medal from the city commissioner all before he even turned 14.

He was a good pitcher too, but we as a country are all pretty aware of how much a batsman's hand is a really important hand in the game, the team depends on it. By the time he turned 19, I had planned to enroll him to play for the Ranji Trophy. I was sure he'd be selected, and we raised him well enough for him to recognize that he was the right amount of confidant, and not a single bit too proud that he'd be able to make it, to make his dreams come true. He was one of the best in the city, definitely on the Top 10 players under 19 for 5 consecutive years. Cricket coaches, institutes and academies used to call day and night to get an opportunity to associate with him. His life's path was set to near perfection.

But one day, before he turned 19, I received a call from his coach and then his friends to visit him at the field. They didn't sound like it, but when I reached there, it turned out to be more serious than I was prepared to face. Vikram had fainted mid practice, he was experiencing fatigue for a few days prior to when it happened, but we never would've suspected it to be anything more than just the heat waves of the summer sun. He was just conscious enough to walk to the ambulance. On visiting the doctor, we were asked to take a blood test. They said it wasn't too serious, but they just had to be sure and asked to speak to me alone, so I asked Vikram to wait outside. And then they said that… that… they found signs Vikram's been facing common symptoms of leukaemia. When I saw him after that in the corridor, he asked me if everything was fine. I looked at him as calmly as I could and with a smile I said, "Son, it's nothing serious, they just said that the blood test would require a heads up so I'm going to make an advance payment at the reception now." He nodded and put his head down with patience and curiosity. And obviously, I was hoping for the test to be negative… we all were and my wife and I prayed until the results came. And then came, what

I consider, by far the worst day in our lives. He was diagnosed with blood cancer.

It was hard for us to believe that someone at that age could even have such an extreme disease like cancer... but the doctors said there was hope for him, as he was quite athletic and after studying his blood sample they were pretty positive that his body would respond fairly well to treatment. But only time would tell what would happen. My wife and I had faith, so we prayed again and thought God wouldn't fail me, or my son, maybe this was a test of my faith, I had never done something to be put out of God's good books.

I saw my son lay there, with a needle up his arm, and shaken from within. A few days into his treatment, Vikram looked nervous, his face had turned into a wax figure next to an open flame, like I had never seen him before, he did show some of it while on stage, but except the stage fright, he had never looked at me this way. I asked if there was something bothering him other than his condition, of course, I assured him that the doctors were positive he'd be cured. He hesitantly, with a squeaky little pinch of doubt in his voice, asked me, "Dad? Please tell me the truth… I'll be able to play again right.. I miss the pitch, and my friends, and I hope the coach will let me practice again." I had nothing but a nod of yes and my smile to offer to my son, and console him that the doctors had asked me to have faith, in modern medicine, in their practical experience and in any lord I prefer worshipping that he'd be cured.

After several weeks of treatment, doctors were able to cure him off it. He had a successful recovery. So, in the happy moment, we got him discharged and arranged for a surprise party while I was picking him up from the hospital. His mother, sister and all his close friends waited at home to celebrate the feast. “My prayers have been answered with a blessing.” I patted myself and was floating on clouds, my happiness was beyond explanation, and why wouldn’t I have been, my son had just beaten death.

And while I was driving him, a drunk driver got onto the wheel. He was driving… at least a 100 kilometres per hour in a luxury car. He was charging right at us and before I could even turn to see his car… We were toppled. His car rammed into ours and we went flying across the road. I survived. My son… Vikram took… his last breath… he passed away… while I lay unconscious just a few feet away from his body. And the drunk driver, from what I later heard, had gotten away safe because of his precious car. I didn't even get to say goodbye to my only son. His mother was worried, she had called me 57 times that night.

When I regained consciousness, my wife was sobbing the bed wet right beside me and I didn't have the courage to ask her what had happened. It took a toll on me, and that’s when I started drinking, vigorously, for months together, uncontrollably. I behaved like a wild animal in the street, untamed and carelessly. I questioned my faith. One of those days, I smashed the bottle of scotch I held in my hand and dragged myself inside a church, and asked God what kind of sick joke was he playing with my life, with our lives, here on earth and what was it supposed to mean to cure my son off of cancer and then take him away from me the second I had the satisfaction of bringing him home safe. What kind of a psychopath was I praying to, to have written my life like it was living hell? I knew I had nothing else left in my life. My daughter, and my wife had grown apart from me, given the state of mind I was in, it was probably for the best at the time for them. I was living in fear and hatred. I told God that if I can't have my son alive, then I'll meet him dead.

I lost all my faith in anything and anyone and spent the rest of my life as a drunk rascal wandering the roads like a homeless person and managed to survive on the bits of leftover that the civilized class today would basically call garbage. Until 9 years later, when I was completely drunk to the top of my head and to the bottom of my soul, about to commit suicide without even being in a state of consciousness about it. I was walking to a bridge to jump and put an end to this preposterous misery of a tale my life had become. Just then, a driver passing me happened to notice me, and as I was almost hit by his car, he stopped. He got down from the vehicle and assessed my condition from the way I looked. He decided to take me in with him despite my violent, threatening, and dangerous disagreement and drove me to a hospital. He signed the forms stating he was my brother and even cleared all my bills. When I came to my senses, I got to ask him, "Why? Why bother? What could you have gained from helping someone as reckless as me? I'm a cockroach of society, I'm worth nothing."

He then told me that he had lost his son to an accident involving drinking and driving. Just two months before he crossed paths with me. He saw me in the condition I was and how I could be a danger to myself and others around me. And that's why he was so quick to help me because he knew… he had seen with his very eyes what people could become, because that's exactly what had happened to his son. His son was fed up with the way his wife treated him, and forced him into a divorce to claim the alimony, and how his dream of a company was failing, and then getting drunk on the wheel had ended his life before he had the chance to realize that he could change. So, this man decided to never let anyone in his sight make a bad decision when drunk, or sober, and to make them understand that they can take the time they need to let themselves heal, to realize the potential they hold and to envision the person they could then become.

That man did to me, what I, with all the faith on Earth, could not have done, in less than a day. And that very day, I promised myself, and decided that I was going to turn my life around. I forgave the person who was responsible for the death of my son. I got back with my wife and daughter. And I started coaching cricket to the children from the school that Vikram studied in who couldn't afford to pay the fee for a private coach. And the most important decision I made was to stick to my faith, despite not believing in an all-powerful, Supreme Being of power. Because that would be wrong of me, for the only creature or creatures if you will, I could have undying faith in, were the very humans I lived amongst, the people that surround me.

After all these years of conducting these talks, and sermons for helping people quit alcoholism, gambling, or any other self-destructive habits they possessed, I never wanted anyone to have faith, or find faith, I simply want them to see, for all of you to see… that all this time that you spend on a habit could be utilized to make something more of yourself, to become someone, more… YOU! To harness the power within your will. Because I don't have to have faith in some deity. I had mine taken away and restored. If I could do it, allow me to help you do it, or at least find a way.

9

BOOK-A-BLESSING

by Naqiyyah Calcuttawala

Like yours, my parents too are sick of my eating habits. Not even one morning passed by when I was not shouted at for not eating my breakfast before going to school (which was probably five months ago when I attended school physically not virtually). Being a badge holder in school, I had been entrusted with a lot of responsibilities. Mostly during recess, I used to work around and did not get time to eat my lunch. I usually ate while returning back home or my friends would secretly have it. This happened regularly and it hardly affected my health because my system got used to this, hence I was the same active person, jumping around, doing work, and getting it done. Never, throughout these years by God's grace have I fainted or had any vitamin or mineral deficiency.

When the lockdown initially started, all was going smooth. But as days passed by gradually situations around me just worsened. At that time, I had zero adversity quotient, no tolerance level and weeping was a necessary element of the day. In fact, my appetite just rose to an unbelievable level. Not that much junk was taken in, but of what I ate normally, it just doubled. I gained so much weight because of which the mirror was the last thing I wanted to look at and this was just unusual because I am a narcissist. A calm and composed person like me would get annoyed at the least of things and I just felt like breaking everything that came my way. This level of anger was just unacceptable on my part. With the ongoing situation that time, plus the additional drama that my close ones made (as though they threw a bomb) just took a major toll on my mental health. It was as if every person disliked my presence around them and I felt as if I was in a lonely land of darkness with no beam of hope that would take me back to the happy and self-satisfied person I was because every limit to a given situation had just been extraordinarily crossed. One day while I was sitting in my room, every negative thought kept coming back to my head and I could not take it anymore. While walking towards the living room, I blacked out. I just collapsed. After fifteen to twenty minutes, I did get my consciousness back, but everything seemed to be blurred. I was trying to eat dinner, but my body just gave up. It started shivering and I felt so choked. At that time also instead of letting me be at peace, I was blamed regarding my eating habits and about the fact that I was malnourished because there was no other reason except for that. But little did anyone know that I had been overeating. No one realized the mental stress that had actually led to a blackout like that. While I rested, I could hear the entire blame game going on. I was held irresponsible and dull for the fact that I went down just once to the shop and that I had caught the virus which was completely false, since I did not even have the slightest of covid-19 symptoms (Indian parents and their misconceptions). In my entire life, that was the first time my body genuinely felt lifeless and it just felt as if it was my last day on earth. It may sound a little unusual, but my grandfather who passed away when I was four years old, appeared before me and held my hand. It did not creep me out, but it just felt that I was already a part of another world. I simply went off to sleep after that, not knowing the fact whether I will wake up the next morning or not. I just gave a very tight hug to my mother and little brother. On waking up the next morning, I anticipated that I would be standing on a bifurcation between hell and heaven but thankfully I was on my bed. With my phone being confiscated, I went pondering around the house looking for something interesting that would productively pass my time. While I lolled around, I came across a book named 'The Unposted Letter' by Mahatria Ra, who just seemed to me as an over smart guy who gave lectures to people about how to be happy and alive. The first thought that struck me when I got my hand on that book was, "This man needs to get a life for himself because the people of our generation will be happy for a moment and the complete opposite in the next moment. Hence, time should not be wasted in giving them lectures on how to lead their life and considering their ego level, this topic is a big no no." Little did I know that this book was all that was necessary for me and that Mahatria Ra, was my angel in disguise and his book, a blessing. Since I was jobless nor could I watch Netflix, the thought of analysing the nonsensical things written in that book occurred to me hence I started reading. My mind was literally blown. Counsellors and other teachers have never been able to impact me in such a big way that a mere book has been able to do. As I read that book, it felt that Mahatria Ra is personally giving me all the solutions to problems that I have never been able to figure out myself nor on the advice of other people. After reading that book I can actually categorize my life into two parts: before the collapse era and after the collapse era. Before I read this book, "professional procrastinator" was my pet name but what I majorly learnt from that book is, "Today is the gift of God unto you. If you disrespect this gift you're simply disrespecting the giver of the gift." Hence now I make sure that today is accomplished to the fullest. Books do involve me a lot, they allure me into all of the happenings, but that is just temporary because after one or two days it just fades. But this book is not any mere book, a blessing is the right word, it has given me a new life, a permanent impact of being the best and strongest version of myself. That author (my angel) has connected with me through pages, I wonder what vibe it would be when he is physically present in front of me. Whenever I feel low the only thing I want to do is read his book because it lifts my spirits and pushes me to do the most and more.

Hence all hardships that led me to such a pathetic state of mind was all worth it because such a wonderful book was on my way and unless I would not have collapsed nor would my phone be confiscated, I would have never been able to come across this book. Everything does happen for a reason and it is for one's own good, which is why patience is the most important factor. It was aptly quoted by Oscar Wilde, "What seems to us bitter trials are often blessings in disguise."

10

TURNING POINT

by Raghavi Shankara Guhan

An eight-year-old Sita jerked out from her dreamland hearing the bell ring signalling the end of her mathematics lesson, thus, the end of school as math was her last lesson for the day. Even without realizing, after receiving her horrible results, she had cried herself to sleep such that the whole lesson had already finished without her teacher having noticed her absence.

She silently packed her belongings in her tiny barbie bag as she walked to her bus waiting to carry her home with slumped shoulders. At that tender age also, she was very stressed because she knew her mother was going to be very upset with her for having lost lumps of marks due to millions of silly mistakes and minor conceptual errors.

She recalled how her *amma*, Sudha had spent weeks teaching and revising concepts required for the test with her. She knew she had let down all the expectations her mother had with her and that made her feel even more horrible. The smiling face of her mother wishing her good-luck, warding off evil eyes came back into vision as fresh tears streamed down her doe-like eyes.

After reaching home, she was greeted with a cheerful smile plastered on her mother's face, but that smile dropped instantly seeing a depressed looking Sita. Sudha immediately got worried as all the worst-possibilities of what could have happened ran through her head because Sita was a bold and outspoken child, so such a scene was very rare to her. Sudha calmed herself, fearing scaring Sita further, as she tenderly held Sita's chin, making her look at her in the eye and questioned: "What happened *kanna*, are you alright! It is not very common to see this balloon-faced Sita is it?" she said trying to lighten the mood, but to no use as Sita did not even seem to pay notice to the words as she was lost in her own worries.

Without replying, head hung low, Sita quietly walked into the house, heading straight to her room, leaving Sudha even more perturbed and worried for the child as to the motherly instinct told her that it was inner conflict that was bothering her child more than any external reason. Nonetheless, she could not pinpoint the cause exactly.

Defeated, Sudha went to carry on with her household chores where the worry for her little Sita was constantly nagging at her from the back. She decided at such times it was only Sita's father, Karthikeyan who could bring out the child from her misery.

Karthikeyan always had a way with his words which would always hold answers to the endless questions of Sita which would mostly render Sudha stunned. Even though most often he also did not know an exact answer, he would always find a suitable reason to give Sita to push the child to find her own answer.

This is what Sita loved about her father, when he had no answers, he would still play with words in a way which would make Sita herself feel lost for words, confused in her own question. With each question she would ask, she would be met with another question that brought her closer to the potential answer.

Sita was a child with exponential potential who would just never stay quiet, talking and asking questions was like a second nature to her making her the apple of the eye of all her teachers as well as her parents. She was a talented singer, graceful dancer, excellent in most of her academic subjects, yes most, except math. If there was something she was bad at, it would be math, and that subject particularly, was the one in which her *amma* excelled.

Since childhood Sita had always heard that she had gone after her mother, so not being good in math was something she couldn't bring herself to believe and constantly overworked herself for scoring in that particular subject, yet not quite meeting her expectations. Probably that was one of the main reasons why she was very disappointed this time, because she and everyone else knew the amount of effort she had put this time.

Even though Sudha was not aware of the worry that was eating away her daughter inside, she knew this for sure, that the wound was possibly so deep that Sita would not share it with her because her child was scared that it might hurt her too. She silently prayed that her husband returned from work early today to settle the turmoil being faced by their soft flower-like Sita.

Sita had switched off all the lights of her room and embraced the darkness. Maybe in that tiny head of her's, she had wanted to hide her tears and make her parents assume her to be asleep even if they were to check on her.

As Sita silently shed her tears of unhappiness the door creaked open to reveal her father who was just back from work.

After hearing about the encounter with Sita from Sudha, Karthikeyan had straight proceeded to meet his daughter after dropping his office items in his room and freshening up. He could guess that it was something to do with the results because on the way back from work, he had met one of his daughter's classmates who was asking him if Sita was alright. Surprised with the question, upon enquiring Sita's friend, he had come to know that the math test results were out. From there he could roughly draw a conclusion himself as to what could have happened.

As he entered the room, Sita could vaguely see him because he was at the door with the hallway on the other side being lit, so his silhouette could be seen even though Sita was surrounded by darkness. She didn't know how he realized that she wasn't asleep. Instead, he switched on the lights using the switch near the door.

The switching on of the lights momentarily blinded Sita as she blinked a few times to get accustomed to the brightness.

He slowly walked towards her, as she in vain tried to quickly brush away the tears that had streamed from her eyes. He silently came and sat beside her on the bed, as he gazed forward. Without looking at Sita, in a soft, soothing voice he asked: "Do you see it Sita?" the puzzled child asked "Huh, Appa I don't understand!?". He again repeated the same question even slowly and softly to make sure she heard him clearly "Do you see it *kanna*?", now Sita was getting curious and confused. She asked him "What *appa*!? See what?".

Finally turning to her he replied: "This *kanna*, this light, this brightness, did you notice how after sitting for a long time surrounded by darkness when suddenly faced by bright light, your eyes automatically close shut as they blink and try to adapt themselves to the change? The light feels piercing initially, but once you're accustomed to them, the very same are the ones which make you see things around you."

Sita felt really very curious to hear his talk, but at the same time confused as to why suddenly he was telling her something like that, so she questioned him, "Wow *appa*, that is something I never noticed, but what relation does it have to me". He replied: "I was talking about light and dark *kanna*, but their teachings can be applied everywhere. Tell me one thing, I know you were depressed with your marks, but were you crying because Amma will scold you or were you crying because you felt you had some conceptual gaps or made silly mistakes?"

Sita embarrassedly looked down and replied, "I was upset appa, but I was more scared of Amma scolding me because she is so good in math, but I am not." He smiled and said: "You are not good now; doesn't mean you never will be. Just like when your eyes are suddenly exposed to brightness when they have been in the dark for long durations they will feel uncomfortable and will automatically make you squint and blink for several minutes to get used to the light, you need to take effort to make you accustomed to the subject. Now you study math for the sake of marks and for your mother, not because you want to learn and understand. But once, you start looking at the subject as a form of knowledge you will automatically fall in love with it. Just like your eyes get used to light, you will get used to math too."

Saying that, he left Sita alone to ponder upon her thoughts. As he proceeded to switch off the light before leaving, she called out to him "Appa, let the room stay lit" to which he smiled as he shut the door behind him.

This left an eight-year-old Sita enlightened. To that tiny soul, it was a turning point in her life. She felt as if she had won a thousand gold medals, because her father's words had really touched her the way they should have.

That day she understood that there is nothing that is technically impossible, yes, for some it might be harder to understand than the rest, but once something is understood, there is nothing more to do at all, as knowledge is a character of life, once fallen in love with, be it math, science, or any other subject it just flows.

25 Years Later

Dr. Sita Karthikeyan was standing at a podium at a medical conference in Singapore standing straight with pride as small drops of tears streamed down her eyes as she completed reciting a part of her life- "Turning Point" to the crowd as form of inspiration to those budding doctors, as she remembered her parent's smiling faces who were staying far away from her, in India.

As she stepped down, soon she was met with crowds of medical students who surrounded her with endless questions and tips for inspiration on how to study and so on. Looking at these students recollected her younger self filled with endless questions and with the drive of serving the society.

She replied to all of them: "When you want something so badly, you will automatically fall in love with it. When you fall in love with something so hard, it will automatically come to you. To excel, all you should not be coming to me with a question on how to score instead, you all should ask how to understand."

This answer confused the students where one of them asked: "But Dr. Sita, how can we not ask about marks when marks define our future? Aren't marks by which we are judged?"

Sita smiled and replied: "Yes, marks are important, and they do play a part in dictating your future, but are they your future? My answer would be no. Your future is dependent on your understanding of what you learn more than digits called marks. When you operate a patient, no one will ask you your medical score, but your knowledge of which vessel to cut and which steps to follow. For success you need knowledge more than marks, remember children, marks are not equal to knowledge, they are just a factor used to determine your degree of knowledge obtained. They, by no means define who you are, so strive for understanding not for winning."

Saying so as Sita exited the conference hall. Her words had the same impact on the students, like a point in her life where her father's words had left such an impact on her.

That day her father had created her 'Turning Point', today, she was creating a 'Turning Point' in the lives of many others.

***

Vocabulary :

Appa: Father in Tamil

Amma: Mother in Tamil

Kanna: Child in Tamil

11

THE TEST DRIVE

by Malvica Sangeetham

Let me ask you a question- what do you do when you develop feelings for someone? You will first go through between fluctuating stages of admittance and denial. Then you will start to feel that it's just a phase and it'll pass away, and then before you even know, you're head over heels in love. Now, let me be practical. Confessing those feelings is a very big task. Some people just keep that little feeling bottled up deep inside a little corner, because it would end up being a really big mess. Some would just feel that saying it out is the best thing to do.

So I decided to choose the next option- well, I had to because he made out that something was bothering me. My next question is- what happens when you confess your feelings to someone? They will either accept you, or not. Am I right? So here's what happened to me. He was very understanding, so he mentioned that it was completely okay, and that I shouldn't feel bad or guilty about this.

Well, it was a big deal for me because I finally thought I'd keep a person all to myself, and that love would not fail me. "You're a very important part of me, I just can't lose a friend like you, but if you feel that it's going to be hard for you, then it's completely your decision. We can still be friends like how we always were, and things will be exactly how it used to be, but I'm extremely sorry because I can never feel this way about you."

Now after this, we became even closer, but we were just friends. People around us thought we were a couple (like literally). Things kept going smoothly, and he was always there for me at any point of time, and at any point of the day. And whenever I'd go sober or start talking about my feelings for him, I must say that he handled me like a pro.

It all looks like everything is nice right? Here's where the storm starts because that's when the twist happens in every story right? One day he came up to me, and he asked me, "Hey, I was just wondering if you can be my follow up." Now I was utterly confused about this, so I asked him what he exactly wants. He gave me a really big explanation about it, so I'll just brief up about what he said. His past relationships have been terrible. So terrible that he wasn't ready for another one. He wasn't prepared for going through that all over again. So was I. If we have a little trial round, like to have a little test drive, we can see how things work out for us, as a couple. It sounded quite legit because we have seen each other's highs and lows in such a way that we can actually make out what's wrong with either of us in a way no one else can. He and I were connected in a frequency so high, that it was unimaginable. Plus, we've lost everything, so there's nothing to lose.

So we made up some ground rules and decided to proceed with this little experiment. It was great, I must say, but as you'd expect, when things happen to go too good for a while, something bad always stirs up. That scene just keeps flashing in my head every time. I kept thinking about why he asked me to do this thing with him, when he's not going to see me from a lover's perspective because deep down he still wants the girl who never made enough time for him. He knew that he's losing track of her, and he kept trying very hard, and that just kept hurting me. When I told him to let it go, he just wouldn't, no matter how much she'd gotten on his nerves. All I can say is he just needs some time to see what is correct for him, but how much time is sufficient enough?

I just can't keep waiting all my life for him. Yes, I love him more than anything, but not at the cost of my inner peace. I'd go to bed every night dreading about this and wake up every morning making up my mind not to give up, and that there's light at the end of the tunnel. You know where the problem is- he doesn't let me go, but he doesn't hold me up tight either. I don't understand what's holding him back from understanding what he actually wants from me. It's just made me stand still. Well the story stops here, but all I know that it hasn't. Only time can disclose what is actually going to happen, and all you can do is just sit back and see what happens.

The Test Drive- Part-II

Time heals wounds. Time makes you forgive. Time gives you closure. Now, how much time are you willing to give? In this fast-paced world, where we expect things to happen as soon as possible, are you willing to give away your time just to know if he's the one? Our fates were playing a dirty game with us. I had reached a point where the 'enough-is-enough' phrase crosses our mind more often. He was right there, and so was I, and so was the girl he had fallen in love with.

Doesn't this look like a quintessential love-triangle? No wonder one-sided attractions sting you real hard. We had started to distance ourselves at this stage, not because we wanted to. But because our situations demanded it. Well, I don't know about how he was handling it, but I was having a really hard time coping up with this. I desperately wanted things to be like before, where we both were carefree and always talked and did the silliest things together.

Apart from that, here's something else that was also bothering me- I had started to think that he might be feeling awkward around me. I had also asked him about this. He just kept saying the same thing he always tells me- that I'm overthinking. Me being his girlfriend could be the wrong decision, but I couldn't lose a friend. I just couldn't handle this. Another thing I had learnt about him was that he had an issue of expressing his feelings, and also that he doesn't talk much. So, all this while, starting from when we met until now, was he just messing with me?

This love story had started with friendship and comedy and had now reached a point where there's a lot of complicated things between us. I was trying really hard to join the dots and attach the missing pieces so that I could get a clearer picture. He'd go and fool around with the other girls for a mere distraction like always, and I got back to being a serious and boring person.

Maybe the test drive was very bumpy. Maybe we just kept slipping off every time we did something for each other. I'd say that college was our culprit. We got so preoccupied with stuff in college, it had become our best excuse for avoiding each other.

Let's take a leap from this really sad phase. College was coming to an end, and he would be graduating in a short while. So I thought, "Hey! We'll be parting ways from each other, so let's end it on a good note". Instead of getting all mushy and gloomy about him not being around anymore, I had decided to bring him a farewell gift. I broke my head trying to figure out what would be a suitable gift for this guy. He had called my phone the day before his convocation. He just kept the conversion very short. "It's my graduation day tomorrow, and I want to spend some time with you before I'm gone."

I didn't sleep that night. I just waited for my D-day to arrive. I had to finish off with some work that day, so I met him along with the others. Boy, I drooled over when I saw him in his graduation robes along with his degree. When we finally had time to talk, I took him to the most deserted area of the college campus for more privacy. Deadly silence first, it took a bottle of coke to break the ice. That was one heart-warming conversation and the most memorable one.

***

I had eventually bought him a gift. And it was the most unusual gift anyone would have ever given. I used to have these pocketbooks where I'd write down things which would give me ideas for my write-ups. In these set of pocketbooks, there was one such book where I'd written whatever I felt for him. This little pocketbook was all about him. I had written little haikus, verses, poetry pieces, love quotes that were all related to him and our relationship. I never knew that I'd give away this book to him one day. A week back, I had decided that I have to move on. Start afresh. This particular pocket notebook was a piece of me. So I thought, why not give away a piece of me to him as a gift? When I narrated this to him, he literally cried. For the first time ever, I had seen this guy cry. No one had ever read anything written in this pocket notebook, and I told him that no one should ever read this. It was between me and him only. What we had was so special, I wasn't ready to share this with anyone. Our story didn't have the ending I had wanted, but it ended on a good note. We still keep in touch. Love wasn't the road for us. It was friendship. And I'm glad to have a friend like him by my side.

I could never be his love, or the girl he wanted to end up with. Life's funny that way. It teaches us lessons in a really uncanny way. Obviously, we don't always get what we want and there's a reason. Our chapter came to end right after his graduation, but it was one hell of a chapter. Our bond, our friendship, everything turned out to be a blessing in disguise, and here's how. I could never be so brave to express my feelings until he persuaded me to. No matter how awkward things got between us, he was there for me. This test drive is one thing I will cherish forever.

12

THE RED ZONE

by Hitesh Kumar Singh

It was dark. The court lights were on. A massive, tensed environment was in the air. Only the sound of black crows could be heard. The water boy was crushing the bottle just because of his great involvement in the match. Even the umpire stood up from his chair for that last point. I got the racket, a shuttlecock, and a bit of nervousness in my hand.

As soon as I stepped back to swing the shuttlecock, a disturbance came from the right side, very soon it became bigger. All of us were watching the big shrubs in the right yard, and within seconds as we heard the first wave of barking sound, we threw everything and ran towards the fence of the park to save ourselves from the German shepherd.

"Robin take him away… please. I was one point away from my 'treat of dessert'." I said out of frustration.

Robin in a casual way said, "Ya, I was just passing by and thought to say hi to you guys."

"Well, hi and bye, okay. Sounds good!" I said in a fraction of a second.

He left. After taking a deep breath I got back to the ground and saw that only my umpire friend was there, and a half-filled water bottle was lying on the ground. After having laughed at the opponent, I took the water bottle, and we went for a walk around the colony.

We were discussing a few comic stories, having a fun time and suddenly after realizing that we had crossed the red line of the colony, Ajay could hardly utter the words and with difficulty he said,

"You ddd...didn't notice we are in the rr... *Red Zone*... be quiet."

I am a science student and don't believe in ghosts or even anything which doesn't have a reason or scientific explanation. Being ignorant of Ajay's delusion about paranormal things and besides him being afraid of speaking in that situation, I started singing. I didn't even finish the very first line and something like a needle squeezed my backbone in a harsh manner. I stopped and turned back. There was no bee, no fly, no insect, nothing was there except my friend, me, and an annoying silence. I was so confused, and I randomly saw a pinpoint fist, he was holding so tightly that his nerves were bulging out of the skin and I could see that with my eyes. It was weird to see him behaving like that. He was swallowing his saliva from time to time. We finally turned one-eighty degree and decided to go back silently. We were taking a bit longer to step ahead so as to avoid any unnecessary footfall. We were breathing so slow so as to minimize the sound in any possible way. It was that weird. We had almost reached the halfway back and suddenly we heard a high pitched, ridiculous, spooky sound something like a cry. Within no time, Ajay ran like a Formula race car. 'Run' was the only word running through my mind. I too ran like hell. I had crossed the red line, still I couldn't stop. My body knew that it was fine now, but my spirit kept me running until I reached the park. I took a breath and went home immediately.

The next day, I got myself ready and went out for some fresh air and to jog a little. I was waiting for Ajay in the park outside our house, but he didn't come. It was strange as he was always standing in the park before I could even enter. I took it easy and didn't think about it much. I got myself ready for the school. I took my bicycle and waited for Ajay to come downstairs so that we could go together.

Ajay's mom politely said, "Son, you go, he won't go to school today."

"Okay" I said.

I went to school without any inquisition, so as to not to be late for the class. My day was getting very unusual as the time passed by. I got back home, ate very little, slept a little and did my assignment quickly to go out for the match.

I went to the park and saw that the match was going on very well with my peers, but Ajay wasn't there. It made my critical threshold wrath come out. It was the tipping highest point of weirdness that I could handle. Soon I was standing on the floor outside Ajay's father's property to figure out the actual scene. I rang the bell, and his younger brother came out.

"Hey boy, how are you doing?" I said with a cheerful voice.

He in a dull voice replied, "I am good but not my brother."

"Why, what happened?"

"I don't know.. he has had a fever since last night and is not speaking much. The doctor can arrive anytime to check him out. Do you know anything?"

I took a little pause just to digest what I heard.

"Ohh, nah! Don't worry. He'll be fine, it happens." I said in a casual way to comfort him.

I acted calm in front of him just to escape from any inquisition about yesterday. I immediately went to the park so as to feel a little bit good. I sat down on the bench and while I was thinking, I saw someone's hand on my shoulder.

"ahhhhhhhhhh" I shouted and fell down.

"hahaha... what happened!"

"What the heck Tarun." I said furiously.

"You seem worried."

"What can I say! Hey, if I am not wrong, you live near the red zone, right?"

"Ya, but obviously I don't go there even in my dreams."

"Can you just tell me more about it!"

"And why do you want to know that? Nobody discusses it, you know that right?"

"Just wondering... I won't tell anyone... Please...Please... Please."

"OK, ok but don't discuss it later."

"Okay, just tell."

It was getting dark and we sat down in the middle of the park and he began...

"They were new in the colony. A man and a woman. Once my neighbour went to their house on the first day to greet them, but they didn't open the door. The second day, one cop was there in the colony, outside their house. My neighbour again went on to investigate the situation and the cop said that he got an emergency call from the house and he added that a woman was found hanging and the man was missing."

My eyes started bulging out at that moment. My mouth opened uninvitedly and he continued...

"From then the house is locked from outside. Nobody goes there, it's the last house and an open area so we almost ignore going there. One week passed and strange things started happening. One of them being, seeing someone in a full 'black bodysuit' after midnight by some "late owls" in our society who studies late night. There could be a possibility that it can be a hallucination as the one who doesn't sleep well can imagine that, but soon more things started happening. On an average twice a month, we started hearing someone weeping, especially when someone goes near that house and specifically it is a woman's cry, from then it is considered haunted and we had marked the red line and that became a red zone."

I got goosebumps. It was getting darker and I felt very uncomfortable after knowing all of it, so I went straight home. I was at home, but my mind was still in the park. I couldn't stop thinking about it. I picked up my phone to distract myself and just then my mom asked me to bring some edibles from the grocery store, so I picked my bicycle and went on.

I pedalled a good distance and suddenly found that I got a swelling on my left foot. I thought I might have hurt myself unknowingly, while playing at school. I ignored it awhile, but soon it became problematic. Now, I had two choices, first was to go back and second, to take a shorter route for which I had to pass by the red zone. I had already covered a long distance and I didn't want to disappoint my mom. Moreover, it wasn't that dark either and the weather was fine, so I decided to take the short route. I almost reached the red line and I saw the weather changing . The wind started blowing. Seeing that I got nervous and sped myself up to a very good extent and suddenly my bicycle chain got off. I applied the brake but my brake calliper system broke and I started moving forward unwillingly. I eventually saw that I crossed the red line, now this time I started panicking. I dragged my foot on the ground to slow my speed and my bicycle got drifted, disbalanced and I fell near the fence of that 'haunted house'. That was literally, literally, tremendously another level of misfortune.

At that moment, I didn't have my mobile and my body was shivering to the extent that I forgot how to stand and for sure that was not because I had fallen down. I could hear my heartbeat. I was not moving so as to make sure that I make no noise, reducing it as far as possible. I thought, if I somehow make it to the open area then I could run from there. I started walking silently that way, despite the wounded leg, it was very painful but there was no other way. I had crossed the halfway and then I heard the scary weird voice. I almost hid myself in the big shrubs there and didn't come out for a few minutes. Again, I heard the voice, but now it was sort of a painful voice. For me, my instinct was telling that it was a real woman's voice, but I couldn't do anything. I came out and while moving forward, through the shrubs, I saw a woman's shadow on the window. Then I saw one more thing which was weird, there was a little garbage around the corner of the garden.

Now my scientific mind popped up and the fear level dropped a little. I thought what if someone still lives here, but it was next to impossible as the door was locked from outside and what if the house is really haunted. My mind was messed with these kinds of thoughts. I was just figuring out what to do and suddenly I smelled something edible. Now, this was enough to prove that someone was inside. I finally planned that I'll go and peep inside and if something goes wrong I'll run and then, I just had to reach Tarun's home.

Finally, I went to the backside of the house, but there was nothing that I could see. From there I got to the right side and I saw one window which was a little open for air circulation. I very carefully and slowly raised my head and what I saw was heart-breaking, shocking, and unbelievable. I saw a lot of things, including a man and a scared, wounded woman.

"Ahhhhhh..." I uttered out of shock which was heard by both of them.

My mind alarmed me to run away from there and so I ran as fast as I could with my wounded leg, but I couldn't escape, and the man came to me and I lost my hope. I closed my eyes and remembered my parents. Suddenly, I heard a metal hitting sound. I opened my eyes and saw the woman being herself (strong), was holding a rod and the man was holding his leg which was flooded with blood.

"Go, call the cops," said the brave woman.

In no time I went to Tarun's home, explained everything, and the police arrived. After investigation, they arrested the man and praised that woman's bravery and appreciated me as well.

Ajay was fine the next day. He was unwell due to the climate change, but mostly because of his delusions. There's no red zone. No red line, now. We went for a walk that evening and when we reached that house.

"Dev, by the way you didn't tell me what you saw." he said.

I said I saw, "A cop dress, full black bodysuit, some drugs, metal, wood objects and a helpless woman with scars" and I solved that mystery… that it's the case of the man doing illegal work, but as soon as the woman got informed about it and asked him to stop it, he abused her physically and mentally. As he came into the colony, He created an impression that something is haunted in this house and thus kept society away from him and the house. He was the one who used to come outside at night in a full 'black bodysuit' just to scare people and he was the only cop who was standing outside their house on the second day of their arrival who told Tarun's neighbour the story about 'woman hanging and the man missing'. He kept the door closed from outside so as to continue his stay without any doubts among the people in the society.

Now, after all that, I don't know about paranormal things, but what I learnt was that - There is… There was… There will… and There must be a good scientific explanation about anything unusual around. There might not be an explanation known for a few of them, but that doesn't mean an explanation for it doesn't exist. This incident made me believe more in myself and my instincts. As a matter of fact, it has been a blessing in disguise!

13

ABUSED?

by Akshaya Kosuri

"Watch out, Myra. Be well behaved and obliging. Do not disobey your grandma and convey her my regards. Have a great time, okay?" Aadhya implied.

"Alright! Later Mama, I've to get going, see you soon, bye bye!" the 15-year-old daughter said in response.

"Call me once you reach home, take care!" Aadhya adds.

They waved goodbye until out of sight, gradually receding into the distance. The alliance they shared was virtuous, radiant, and noteworthy, a sheer delight. Patently, Aadhya's work as a positive motivational influence procured notoriety, her splendid work-life balance, consistently pleased Myra. Perpetually, the family captivated idealism and glee. Simultaneously, their journeys began in the opposite directions, with Myra visiting her grandmother after four long years and Aadhya wending way to her chores. Under an overcast grey sky, the colours of winter unroll, each hue darker and sumptuous. Myra ambled through the slender track, either side cemented with a stretch of glazed cobblestones, the path sparkles like sugar underfoot, and the glaze arouses her. The vicinity seemed authentic, an exuberant nature with high spirited skies, woods, and soil. A door left ajar casts a silvery beam into the crisp night.

Myra shoves the door and it swung open with ease, an aroma of her favoured cuisine streamed past her and there she was, her grandmother, laughing as if she were a child. Her wrinkles were endearing, and the eyes evinced her soul, a profound pool of apprehension, an ocean of buoyant woe. Passion turned her eyes into orbs of the brightest fire, unravelling her strength. The residence was brimming with vintage treasures and in a while, Myra was prone to snooping in the closets and behind closed doors. Correspondingly, she uncovered a box of her mother's old letters and chronicles with a thick layer of dust. She was definite that the lives of her parents were fairly perfect and exemplary, bustling in the joys of accomplishing their parental duties. Never had she ever pictured they had confidential thoughts or intricate feelings. Myra was put forth with a gateway into her mother's notions. She began to be inquisitive if she wanted to flick through or if it would be a privacy violation to read it. Yet, Myra initiates reading with curiosity and she immediately wished she hadn't, not because the letters contained anything scandalous, but because they clued her into a reality, her mother had distinctly shielded her from. Myra runs through her mother's inscriptions, with a heavy sigh, she sojourns into antiquity.

"In my vulnerability I found my vigour. My mother. I derived solidity from the potent woman of my existence. She had been tested by life's unpredictability. The night was faltering, a visual tranquillity. The anecdotes of that darkness echoes in my soul and bustles about my mind. My mother sprawled on the sack, blood leaching beneath her skin, bones splintering. His hands clenched around her throat. Her chest begins to tighten, ravenous for breath. Regardless of how, we accustomed waking up to the sound of breaking glass. My dad's a trace of an Alcoholic. It's how I fell victim to these bruises and theoretically, my self-induced scars. The camouflaged brokenness that solely an individual exposed to abuse could contend, augmenting blighting insecurity and inhibition.

The phrenic scars are an attenuating facet in the serenity of domiciliary life; they provoke agony that could only be described on the inside. Nights where I lay in my bed, lending an ear to the blare of quarrelling. My father would initiate condemning her, resulting in shrieks. She cried and he convulsed, while I shoved my face into the toy stuffed bear my five-year-old body was muffled around. Aadhyaaaaaa! Aaaaa-dhhhya-aaa! Repeatedly, I would overhear her screech my name between whacks. The first time I recall it happening, I was 5 years old. He was smacking her. He was thrashing her; I could apprehend the uproar of his fist as it strokes my mother's body. My mother was being abused and I was not aware of what to do. I didn't know how to help her. I was helpless and incapable. I would sit in my room and hear her shriek or stand by the shut door with my palm against it. I was in fear, guilt, and helplessness, and I let myself hover in the moment until it was over. It occurred before my eyes.

By some means my five-year-old self assumed that if I myself was not being smacked, then I wasn't affected. But I was, and I am. Home was a dark silhouette of my father. Every detail of my mother's persona was denigrated and evaded. She was summed up unworthy, less than nothing, not even as cherished as an entity exploited. Every gaze that blew in her way was entwined with contempt and annoyance. Every nosh she was flung was demarcated and restrained. Bruises and Trauma, I reckon that's what we receive for persisting voiceless. As I lay my eyes on my mother, coursing tears lustrate her red cheeks, beguiling skin was ashen and pallid, almost anaemic. The sorrow drained through us, it whizzed through every cell of our anatomies. I didn't know if she even recognised that she's putting up with both physical and mental abuse. I would envisage and be hopeful of my mother leaving and I would leave with her too, fleeing the violence.

No matter how dark and dense the storm was, I did scamper back with the wide eyes of a child, confused yet hiding the fear. Two beings whom I loved with all my heart would cross swords as I witnessed it. Each desired to know whom I loved more, but in truth there was no such distinction. It seemed unfeasible enduring the groove. It is tremendous to recall. After all, this was our life. I wasn't a child anymore. Perhaps in reality, it was my parents who acted up like little ones, disputing over something until it broke and even then, they prosecuted, not thoughtful or considerate for the damage they inflicted. It was strenuous. Probably, she believed he would alter, modify, and change, or on the face of it, she entertained the idea of changing him. Little did she know she cannot develop or adjust someone who neither sees an issue, nor the consequences in their actions and deeds.

The gut-wrenching, awful regimen subsisted relentlessly and remained for a long time. Life was never facile with Mom and Dad, but after they got divorced, it was hell, a purgatory. There is so much that goes into becoming and being a mother. I could attain glimpses of my mother crying her eyes out yet, she walked up to me and smiled, it's arduous. She was invariably a woman of ideal strength. Once, as I was entreating him to stop, I recall him slapping me right away. Possibly, this was the trigger for my mother to evaluate a divorce. It was then my mother told herself, she could not change him while he didn't have in view to change. She confronted the fear of not being able to make it on her own, terror of her little one meeting with an adversity from the divorce and terrified about the finance. From self-denial to acceptance and from facing her fears to positive self-talk, she nourished herself. She desired to see her child happy, yet it is hard to raise a happy child if she was not happy herself.

I was about eleven, it was after the divorce, my mother perceived that in the end she could be the only one giving her child a happy mother. Strength grows in the moments when you think you can't go on, but you keep going anyway. Nonetheless, every time I set eyes on a snipped flower; I knew how it was perceived. It had no roots at all, nothing to anchor it into the world, even so, it was looking forward to laying out its beauty, to flourish and warm the hearts of others. No one could ever visualise or get a glimpse of my vulnerability; they could not sight the roots I lack. In the concrete, countless individuals never escape or abscond their childhoods, not in actuality. To some extent, a part of them just doesn't feel shielded in the grown-up world. Commencing from being a little girl up until I was in my early twenties, I intuited the feeling of negligence. I felt inconsequential and trivial.

As I grew into a woman, life took on a new denotation, a collection of choices. I am a legacy of two repudiates, abuse, and desertion. Conceivably, I was in a frolic that I was not called for. My father was in our life one day and scooted the next. My mom and I spent a year reworking and adapting, it was resilience. My father in the company of his new wife was expecting a baby, reassuring us with his actions that he's moved on. The following and final instant I saw him was after a handful of years later, in a courthouse where he validated his authorities away. Being an adolescent, I perceived facts as a fault of mine. I didn't quite decipher what I had done to live a life like such.

I was constantly trying to acquit myself perfectly around my mom. I was worried that she would leave me, too. When guilt makes an appearance, it grasps me down the old decaying intrusive path. I wanted to repulse to walk it, put myself on that I am the person I demand that I be. It is veracious what they say, "Those who don't learn from history are doomed to repeat it" and I couldn't cope with a thought like that. There's a sort of exhaust that stands in need of a good night's sleep, and another that requires so much more. For me, one evolved into the other. Eternity succeeding, as I glance at my mother, alluringly she would flicker her eyes, acquiescing her eyelashes to hover like the wings of a butterfly. Her eyes were modestly spellbinding, they lit up, and I could apprise that a million new ideas and objectives were streaming through her brain. She had witnessed something pristine, something astonishing, like I knew she would and now she is as eager, hopeful as ever.

Her smile was the prepossessing thing I've glimpsed in a while, for it perpetuates to my eyes and deep into my soul. In the wholeness of time, eventually, she seemed happy, genuinely content. Being a single parent grew my mother stronger than ever before, besides, I acquired knowledge of appreciating independent women, while raised by one. I didn't want to prick up my ears when people told me I could knock the walls down if I tried. I didn't want to hang on someone's words anymore. Situating one foot in front of the other is not as serene as it appears.

I was worn out and fatigued of hugs and the well-intentioned words, owing to the fact that nothing could heal me, but myself. Depression is an ocean, the curative I have comprehend for it is a substantial love of self. None are intrepid enough to put in picture to you about this ocean; you are compelled with uncertainty to dive to the verge by yourself. You must be subjected to the agony of learning how to amble by yourself. Nevertheless, when you've been through it, you are unconfined to come upon your heaven. You are liberal to sense content and grow pleasingly with instincts for the succeeding hours of light and days of life. Amidst the scars, hassle, misfortunes, will emerge the indestructible souls, for there is the potential to kiss goodbye and move on with certainty. The suffering is my strength.

Despite the fact that I sprang from a heinous site, was raised among barbaric conditions, and came to terms with brutality and finally, I gained an understanding of life. I wasn't born for that; we didn't set foot on to a heavenly body of such virtue to live attenuated to cope with life's tempests. It is never the event or the circumstances that defines us, yet the attitudes and manners of the ones involved. Though these things are never effortless, we do get to make up our mind or choose our response and how receptive we are to learn the enlightenment and emerging much more empathic than we were ever before. I am obliged for all the shut trails for they have redirected me from tracks that weren't meant to be. If I weren't deserted sinking, how else would I have risen?

As glistening tears cleansed my eyes, undoubtedly it cleansed my intuition. If I wouldn't endure the agony, how else would I discern the virtuous? I moulded my path from place to place, now I discover where I belong. I broke down, only to elevate and to do better. I watched the gloomy clouds through the sun and the walls fall. Yet, when all was done, I gained the vitality to hold them high, turning a blind eye as I stroll by. I was shattered and broken, but in the course of time I realized it was a blessing in disguise."

With a heavy sigh, as the tears glided from Myra's unblinking eyes, she kissed the cover. They say, the more a daughter knows the details of her mother's life, the stronger the daughter and eventually Myra realized the concept is verifiable. The respect and love she had towards her mother and grandmother grew enormously. With Certainty, she knew reading them had undoubtedly inspirited her. As the stars shimmer, the night takes on an aura of insight, she wraps herself in profound sleep.

Aadhya wasn't efficient in constraining what was done to her but was effective in choosing how to overcome it. She wasn't a victim for sharing her story, but a survivor casting light and warmth with raging courage. Ultimately, A diamond is a chunk of coal that handles cuts, stress, and pressure exceptionally well. The struggle we undergo often puts us on the path to the best things that will ever happen to us.

14

THE LOST GIRL

by Deepshikha B

It was an overcast day, the rain lashed down the rooftop and a strong gust of wind blew against her face. She as usual, completely lost in herself and writing down her unnamed desires and thoughts. It was as if her brain barely knew about serotonin anymore.

She never tried introspecting herself or maybe never found someone. This wasn't her at all. She was just an 18-year-old lassie, instead of having gloomy feelings all she had was scars. Scars that were never meant for her. Scars were given to her by a father, a brother, a son, and a husband. And she lived in a place where her feelings and self-respect was tactlessly cursed and crushed. A place where she got a new moniker every day, for someone it might be rosy and for someone honey. And the society, they almost preferred calling her a slut. All she had was lights with terrible nights and disintegrated happiness. Even though she might give them a call, she self-respects losing strength and fall. Even before bleeding for menstruation, her vagina had bled for the vicious demons called humans.

Where the shimmer on her attire was bright enough to make her lose sight of her childhood. For her, living a normal life was just elusive and she accepted it thinking it was all written in her fortune.

And on one fine cloudy day, she as usual, imprisoned in the shackles of her disguise and sorrow, observes a miasma created on the footpath through her window. And by the time she discovered what was happening, she observed a man running with bleeding bruises all over his body. And finds him screaming, that he'd do anything to stop his love going away from him and that he wouldn't survive without it, cause it was the only purpose for him to live.

She didn't know what he wanted to explain, but what caught her attention was the word 'love'. This put her into deep contemplation as to how far a person can go for his love.

For her, this word was something unfettered. She was completely astonished. And for the first time, she didn't forbear herself from thinking about something new. Just the thought of love made her gallant and she realized that she was just living with a façade. Now all she wanted was to triumph over her helplessness.

The old wooden window before her was like a fae door that would begin with a journey through the door and end the battles that she had been fighting for all these years. All she had to do was to break open it and go forward. That's exactly what she did, showed sheer audacity and jumped through the window, and cantered toward "finding fortune from her misfortune". Alas, she was in love," love with freedom".

In just a wink of an eye, she was out of a dreadful nightmare. It was as if she had just discovered a Bohai. A place where she'd no longer be a toy for a masochist. A place where people don't get transfixed, a voyeur on the swell of her buttocks. She was the happiest person right now, but she was too naive to fathom that happiness was just an illusion for a girl like her. She was too naïve to understand that a person need not be touched to be abused, but just a dagger look would tear apart her clothes and make her bleed due to the injury caused to her pride and self-respect. This outer world was not as gratifying as she thought. It was a *'MAYA'*.

And she had deep-rooted this thought that *'DIAMONDS ARE MADE UNDER PRESSURE'*. And was ready to take any kind of pressure to get her hard work reflect as bright as that of a diamond. Every time she tried climbing up the tree of success the misogynist in the society was always there holding an ax to cut it down.

Now she was just a free little bird who had broken out herself from the cage of disguise. She was out in this world to broaden her horizons. She wasn't among them to get lost in 'his' name but was here to create one. She wasn't here to create history but was here to change the present. The curses given to her by the hypocrite were just like the Horcrux, making her beliefs and desires immortal. And then she realized *"this world was not killing her but was making her even stronger"*. Strong enough to combat, strong enough to fall, strong enough to win.

With these struggles, she had tarnished and sabotaged the weak, helpless girl in her and gave birth to a fighter. A fighter who was strong enough to unleash her words, her thoughts, and desired a better world for herself and people like her. And one fine day she was successful in doing so. She was successful in making an abode for all the helpless souls. A place where they helped people "Find fortune from misfortune". A place where no scars were given by a father, a brother, a son, and a husband. But a place where all their bruises were healed by love. Love given by a mother, a sister, a daughter, and a friend.

The above story has not been written only for publishing purposes, but also to spread awareness against the patriarchal belief.

"WOMEN DON'T DO IT UNDER PLEASURE, BUT MOSTLY DO IT UNDER PRESSURE".

15

ARNI

by Likhitha Kotika

This story is a speech, rather, I would say a live one to one talk with a crowd of over ninety thousand school kids, two thousand teachers and principals approximately and millions of people watching on TV at NEPN, Ahmedabad.

NEPN, The National event of pupil's nourishment is an annual event that happens in the country's biggest open cricket stadium where pupils from all over India gather together and different types of creative competitions are held to identify the unique talent of every kid.

This is that speech which made a huge impact among the audience, especially on me. It was just a speech to the audience, but a true and tough phase of her life which she can never forget. In her words, that phase is one of the reasons that made her a stronger person to face the real world.

***

18th FEBRUARY, WEDNESDAY

MOTERA STADIUM – AHMEDABAD

THE NATIONAL EVENT OF PUPILS NOURISHMENT

"This scene will definitely be there in my movie..." said an eight-year-old to herself on her way to school thinking of some incident. She didn't even know how movies are made and what all it takes to make a film, but always used to say this line each and every time she found some situation interesting. She always used to look at situations in a third person's point of view or rather should I say 'theatre audience' point of view. She has built a big fort of dreams called cinema out of her desire and passion towards films which served as the strongest bricks to her enormous fort even before she realized what she was thinking about. She just hid this entire thing deep inside her heart and never expressed to anyone.

That eight-year-old has come a long way from dreaming to directing a movie to winning the nation's heart through her unique and different style of movie making today.

Let's welcome the chief guest of the day Miss. Arni

Arni's Speech

A very good evening to one and all... Firstly, thank you for such a wonderful introduction Mona... I'd like to congratulate the management of all schools and teachers for their efforts in bringing such a huge number of students to this National Event of Pupils Nourishment. I feel so privileged to be at this event today.

Umm… When the NEPN team approached me asking to speak at their event as one of their chief guests; I was both happy and blank at the same time. I didn't know what to say to such bright little kids here. I only could picture them wanting to listen to stories.

So, I'm not going to give any motivational speeches or quotes today. Instead, let's all talk today. I've some stories to tell you too...

Hey kids! Can I get a 'Hi' from you..?

The kids replied together, 'Hiiiiii....'

Are you ready?

Great! This is the story of a girl.

Once upon a time, There was a very active and naughty girl in a school. Just like the one who always gets caught doing mischievous things. She used to play pen-fight with the boys, compete with them on kicking the wall leaving a shoe mark and what not... She used to participate in all kinds of extracurricular activities too. Teachers referred to her as a very talkative and naughty girl but never got to complain as she got decent grades in studies.

She was always told that studies are the only way to succeed in life and in addition to that, her mother being a teacher made sure she studied well to keep her reputation up among her colleagues. The girl blindly believed in those words and studied hard for the first position but got the second position mostly. Her parents were quite happy, and she was also made one among the class leaders.

But, as she grew older and reached high school, her grades went down. People started treating her differently and she couldn't take it. There was a drastic change from the time when she used to get good grades to the day when her friends and teachers treated her like a 'duller' (it's a name given by the teachers to the students who score less than their expectations.)

Days passed on and summers were coming soon... In those days there were half-days during the summers every year. The happiness of going home half-day at noon, mom feeding lunch while we watch our favourite cartoon and then taking a nap… That feeling was heavenly.

Just like any other child, the girl was also eagerly waiting for the half-day school announcement. But her happiness lasted just for a few seconds when her teacher continued to announce the list of - so called 'dull students' who should stay back in the afternoon while the rest of the A group students can go home. She was almost in tears when her ma'am took her name in that list. In those days having their name in a B/C group was a big insult to the students.

Tears were now rolling down her cheeks.

The girl went to her class teacher and asked, "Teacher, why is my name in the duller list? I am not that dull at studies to stay back ma'am," she said.

"Your biology teacher has put your name in the list. She thinks you need extra classes for revision," said the teacher.

She couldn't understand why a B/C grade student always gets humiliated in that way. The girl never got to go home early during that summer. She always had to stay at the school for extra revision classes with the other dull students.

The next year, 10th standard...

It was mid-July and one day 'the girl' and her best friend Meenu were sitting on the same bench. It was biology class and Meenu was the favourite student.

The teacher seeing the girl and Meenu sitting together immediately after entering the class told... "Meenu! What are you doing sitting next to her? Go sit somewhere else, otherwise you'll end up becoming like her."

No one in the class got what 'becoming like her' meant. The girl was shook and deeply hurt by her words. She couldn't stop crying throughout the day. Her mom was told that she is useless and will end up failing boards after which her mom had to quit her job just to concentrate and take care of her studies.

As the days passed, she gradually got transformed into a very silent and mysterious girl from a naughty, active girl. All her confidence shattered and drained with such incidents. Within no time, she turned out to be an introverted girl who sat alone on the first bench, always in her own world, scribbling her thoughts every now and then on a piece of paper and grew apart from her friends too.

The only thing that was always on her mind which she never expressed to anyone was... "I should get my place back. I want to be in the top 5 again. I can't let these people treat me that way."

She started working harder and harder than she used to before...She scored descent marks and gradually her grades started increasing to 9.2 GPA until pre finals.

The strongest pillar that made this happen and who always got her back was her mother. She quit her job just for her, kept on encouraging and motivating the girl to get her self-confidence back. Slowly, the girl started believing in herself all over again.

The girl, who hated to stay back at school in the afternoon during summers, went to school after every board examination just to study and give her mother a small break from her studies. Finally, the boards were over. She slept for hours, enjoyed, and watched TV for the fullest for more than a month.

After almost one and half months, the board results were out. She woke up early in the morning and went to the nearest temple, returned home and was waiting for the results. She neither had a system with internet nor a smart phone at home then. Her dad called from his office to her mom's phone and asked for the hall-ticket number. The girl could hear her own heartbeat increasing for every second while her mom read out the hall ticket number 1-4-3-7-1-0-6-3-2-1… She scored 10/10 in all the subjects leaving social studies in which she scored 9/10. Her total grade points on a whole were 9.8 out of 10. She didn't top but stood in second place. She was a bit sad for not scoring 10 GPA but was also happy to see her parents happy. She had a time lapse memory of the past 8-9 months, all those discouraging words from the teachers and some peers were echoing in her mind.

Their mentally torturing statements which got her self-confidence down were wrong. She was so happy to prove the ones who told that she could barely pass and got her place among the top 5 again. Yet, somewhere deep inside heart, she knew there was something missing. She was still silent and blank. She tried to behave normal. She wanted to study, have friends and chill with them but still felt incomplete. A part of her heart remained an unsolved jigsaw puzzle. Nothing seemed to work out. She used to watch at least 3-4 movies per day. One day suddenly found herself sitting in front of the TV and laughing out like hell. That day, she found her heart's missing piece.

She's the person who comes out when none is watching. She's the naughtiest when she's with her family when she is not afraid of being judged. From that day, she started being herself not only around her family but everywhere. She no longer felt the need of hiding herself behind an introvert.

That girl who tried to hide herself behind an introvert mask is the girl standing in front you today and her name is

Arni. Yes, that's me… I turned into an introvert when I was judged for the first time, felt numb and horrible.

I now know the value of hard work, happiness, being optimistic and most importantly being myself.

If I hadn't gone through that phase of my life, I'd have never known the value of many things in my life.

I feel my mother is the kind of blessing to me during that phase and if I hadn't had her during that phase of life, I'd have lost my life… I may have ended up taking wrong steps. Whatever I'm or however successful I'm today it's all because of my mom and of course my dad who never stopped being supportive through thick and thin.

On that note, today I'd like to conclude my speech with a small yet very important piece of message that you should learn as a moral of my story...

Dear students,

You might find yourself in similar situations where your teachers and peers might judge you and make you feel humiliated knowingly or unknowingly. Never ever develop any hard feelings towards anyone, not even towards yourself. Always believe in yourself and you'll definitely find someone who would support you just the way I had my parents. You all are very special and talented. Every person in this world is unique and has one's own talent. Find yours and achieve the greatest heights possible through your talent. All the best!

Dear parents,

Please keep a check on your kids. Try to find out what they are going through in their personal life, be it good or bad.

You'll get immense happiness and satisfaction if they're okay and doing good.

If at all you find that something is not right, then please deal with them positively. Help them. Let them know that you have belief in them. None can help them better than you. Making your child a better person is all in your parenting.

And last but not the least...

Dear Teachers,

I request you, please don't ever discriminate or differentiate among your students. Identify the talent in every child and help them improve as a person in such a way that the society starts to recognize them as a better person. The only profession in this world which has the power to make or break a child's future, personality and self-confidence is 'teaching'. That's the reason we Indians treat it as the representative of God.

On a whole, I'd request all of you not to shatter and break when you face any kind of hard times/struggles. Instead, find that ray of hope which becomes your blessing in disguise and helps you move on with all the strength in life.

I thank NEPN for taking up the responsibility of today's generation which is going to be tomorrow's future and appreciate all your efforts in organizing such a huge event so efficiently.

Thank you.

As soon as Arni ended her speech, after a few seconds of silence, there was a big round of applause and standing ovation from all the audience including her co-speakers and chief guests.

There will definitely be something good in every difficult situation and that good is to be found by ourselves and to be worked on. One's right way of utilizing that minute good thing will make the person's life happy, successful and will be one's BLESSING IN DISGUISE.

16

RISE FROM THE ASHES

by Lakshmi Sai Kumar

The world consists of various kinds of people and each individual is different in their way and there are a specific set of individuals who enjoy adventures. Now if I think of it, all individuals are connected through a dynamic adventure that varies from person to person, this is a kind of adventure where individuals rely on their human emotions more than decisive thinking and every individual including myself are in an adventure, wherein some individuals might agree with me whereas there are a certain set of individuals might disagree that life is a never-ending adventure, but it's all in the perspective which they pursue. Now let's dive into an interesting person who is about to teach the importance of getting up from failure and fighting to reach one's goals.

On a bright day as the sun was shining a little boy was born with a loud cry, acknowledging his presence in the world. The days were passing nice and well and the curious little boy Alex with a lot of ambitions and dreams was entering into his first phase of learning in the beautiful adventure of life.

The first day of school is a beautiful experience in everyone's life and the day has finally arrived for Alex. He walked through the doors of the new beginning and was excited to make some friends and fortunately, he made some friends. School days were going really nicely for him, as Alex was very excited for his school life to go as planned and as a good side of the coin, he was enjoying his life to the maximum extent as everything was going as per planned and then, he trusted his friends with his life and he was enjoying spending the most of the time with friends and out of the blue, a day has arrived when Alex was least expecting it, the day when he got split up from his friends as misunderstanding rose which led to arguments which had their effects and then he started feeling the worst effects of the not having his friends along and by the time he realised the friends left the country and tried in all possible ways to connect to them, but all his efforts have gone in vain and he was depressed and the family made him come through his depression and from that moment he was pretty much attached to all his family especially his grandfather who was the world to him and he was the only one to trust all his insights regarding his goals.

As time flew past his happy moments and the day such came wherein he couldn't perform well in his academics as he took academics for granted and was enjoying the happy moments in his life and that is the first time he faced a major setback in the career and he was devasted with the performance he put forth and was in agony because of all the promises he had made and was struggling and ignored everybody and started to feel sorry but then to get back on track he started taking interest in sports as a diversion from his pain and he got his focus back and started playing football for the team and started performing great on double fronts.

Then he was moving forward with a lot of anticipation and was looking forward to a match against his toughest opposition in the tournament wherein he injured his right leg and was in a lot of pain and started to feel depressed but out of sheer determination, he pulled himself together and started playing the game despite his injury helped the team but couldn't win the game for the team which was his second set back and this time he was not that disappointed because he gave his best in the worst condition possible. But the disappointment was there no matter what because he was not able to pull his team through the finishing line.

After failing to reach the finish line then, it was the same repeat which had happened when he had some arguments with his friends wherein He couldn't contact them and then started to focus on understanding people and trying to motivate the people around him who would need the motivation to understand how to go through a certain phase just using a small trick and logic.

Then the days were going on nice and on a happier note. Alex got a call from one of his friends who he had lost contact with and then as soon as the call was done Alex was on cloud nine and he was at his best times and then he saw Ruchi from his college and she came to him and congratulated him for his effort in the football and then their friendship started on a happier note.

The days were going nicely and one day Alex thought and decided to propose to Ruchi on the day and he made his preparation and just as he was about to propose to her, she called him and asked him to meet her and then Alex was very happy and decided to propose her as soon as he saw her. But the day turned out exactly the opposite as he saw his friend and was in mild surprise as she announced that she was in love with his friend.

Alex stated he was very happy for them and reached home with a low face and Alex's father noticed and asked him if everything was alright. He hugged him and started crying his heart out and after a while, he went to his father and he narrated what happened at Ruchi's place.

After a while, Alex quoted saying "Dad! She may not belong to me anymore but I'm glad she is happy and that's what all matters and I have decided to start focusing on my career and I promise I never take anything for granted."

Then it took a while and he started snapping out of it. He started focusing on a new front in his career development and he got stuck with another harsh blow. This was his biggest as he lost his grandfather which was a devasting blow as he was frozen in a time phase as it was the last thing he was hoping to happen. All of sudden the days were moving very slowly for Alex.

As days were passing He was too much taken over by pain that he forgot about himself and started to live his life in pain and forgot about all the passions and dreams which he had and started leading a mechanical life, killing all his curiosity and later he graduated from high school. And started pursuing a course of his interest.

As time passed He started getting normal, he started to reach back to himself and was enjoying each bit of his life again. Soon after recovered from the devasting incident which almost took 3 years for him to get back into his senses. After finding himself again, Alex started to work on a dream project.

As each perspective has its merits as well as demerits and it doesn't mean that only one perspective is right there might be more than one right perspective, which made things more complicated for Alex but due to his never give up attitude and sheer will, he overcame all the hardships, rose like a phoenix from the ashes and completed his dream project and showed the world hard work is might to overcome difficulties and rise to the top again. And that is the success story of Alex and every one of us might relate to the hardships we face but we generally ignore them because we don't pay attention to mental health. Then Alex started working on his dream project of floating up in the field of artificial intelligence and his motive after been through a lot by himself, He decided to dedicate some proportion of his profit towards educating people through his company about the mental health-related issues and improve the standard of living and making people around the world stay positive and stay happy. However, he has experienced a lot of professional hurdles and with his never give up attitude he is fighting through all the difficulties.

Life is a wonderful adventure and everything in this wonderful adventure happens for a reason, however, life is drastically different from any other adventure because in life we rely on human emotions, and every choice we make, we will have a different effect, it might be directly or indirectly on the adventure. Even though it is very difficult we have to accept the adventure as it comes, that is the beauty of life. It allows us to make certain choices that will alter our lives but not everything that happens will be in our control.

Nevertheless, it is easier to tell than to perform it and it is very important especially in the modern world, more than ever before we have to take care of our mental health as it is very crucial and there is no such thing as perfection and no person is perfect. Every individual in the world has a problem and every individual has some merits and demerits whenever you're low on motivation think of the great people like Steve Paul Jobs, Albert Einstein, and many more who had difficulties just like us but what made them great was the attitude after been hit by an unseen disaster.

And always remember it is never late to start over because realization helps in achieving greater things. There is no stopping you if you're committed towards something as the saying says “Luck favours the brave”. Most Important thing whenever you are low always accept help because sometimes help is more valuable which even the money can't buy us and sometimes all we need is a chance which can always be “A Blessing in Disguise” which can turn anyone’s life upside down with the choices one makes.

As the choices we make leads us to a position which is all based on the routes we choose, so whenever you’re in a crossroad and yet to make a choice in what you are about to do, do not rush and regret the decision, but wait.. take a pause and replay your options and if you are still confused ask your heart because it will never let you down.

17

WAS THAT MY FAILURE?

by Sucharan Reddy

Geetha stepped into her secondary education in an ordinary coaching centre, to grail the stoutest course MBBS. It has been her lifelong dream to become a doctor.

It was the Orientation Day at her college.

"Let's go, it's nine already. The meeting would have started," Geetha's mother uttered. Geetha was quite nervous, but her charming face covered it all. "The inauguration would be completed by now," she frowns.

She and her family members were late by twenty minutes.

A tall bald man approaches them with a refreshment drink in his hand. "And you must be the ranker everyone's talking about. Geetha, right?"

"He must be the principle," Geetha's brother Ram whispered in her ear.

She adjusts her voice. "Yes sir, I am Geetha."

"You have an impeccable academic record. Getting a seat in this college is a different ball game altogether, else it would be really hard for your parents to send you here." The principal's expectations from Geetha were sky high.

"Our daughter will not let you down," says Geetha's father.

"I expect the same from her." Saying this, the principal went away to have a word with the other board members.

Negative thoughts start approaching inside her head.

"Will I be able to do it?"

"Did I make a mistake choosing this?"

"What if I don't complete my degree?"

The emerging dreams of her parents and the trust of her principle made her think if she was even cut for this. With a lot of courage and credence in her, Geetha took a step forward to accomplish what she had started.

***

Shalini and Midhun were deeply engrossed in a conversation.

"Come on Shalini! Aanya sounds like a really nice name."

"No. I like Aabha." Shalini sounds very adamant.

Midhun could never say anything that would upset Shalini. So, he decided to play fair.

"How about we toss a coin and decide the name?"

Shalini agreed to Midhun's idea.

"Alright. I'm choosing tails."

Midhun tosses the coin. Waiting for it to fall on his hands, the coin slips and falls on Shalini's three-month-old pregnant belly.

"Our baby chose the name, she likes Aabha." Shalini smirked towards Midhun in a state of complete happiness.

"Aabha. Sounds better than your name," says Midhun as he playfully teases his wife.

This baby was their good luck charm. Midhun didn't want to lose another child. He could never bear to see Shalini fall into depression again. After three failed miscarriages, this was their only hope for happiness.

Meanwhile, Aabha kept listening to all the conversations happening between her mom and dad.

"Dad selected quite a good name for me, but Aabha isn't so bad either."

"Hey everyone! It's my third month here." Aabha has been waiting eagerly to meet her parents.

"You'll never imagine how happy we are right now." Shalini feels through her stomach as Aabha kicks with excitement.

"You'll never imagine how lucky I'm to have parents like you."

"I know that my parents can't hear me right now, but I still want to talk to them."

***

Around five semesters have passed. MBBS is a hard nut to crack, but Geetha made it possible with her talent and charm.

Things were not the same as they were in the first year as Geetha's family had hit a financial crisis. All their relatives and close friends who knew about this didn't want to lend them money as they didn't believe that they would be paid back.

Meanwhile, Geetha's brother Ram had gotten into the Indian Military Academy in Dehradun.

"As Ram chose to join the army, he wouldn't be needing much financial support for his career as I do." Geetha started to think about dropping off so as to take up a job to financially support her family.

One busy morning, Geetha's mother and father get into a heated argument.

"What have you done?"

"Something I should have a long time ago, for our family." Geetha's father reluctantly hands over their property papers to settle all of their previous debts and for Geetha's education.

"Was there no other way?"

"I had to do this for our children's future. There was no other way." Her father walks out of the room and heads to meet his friends in the neighbourhood.

Geetha heard this conversation her parents had, from behind the wall and hurried up searching for a part time job in secret to manage her regular expenses.

***

Now, coming back to Midhun and Shalini.

It's the fourth month now and something unusual happened.

"Oh my God!" Shalini groaned with pain.

"What is it?" Midhun approached her in a hurry.

"I just felt something."

Aabha was full of energy. She has started kicking.

Her kicks made Shalini shed happy tears.

Aabha was very excited to give the first feel to her parents and she started kicking rapidly with caution so that her parents enjoyed the first kick by placing their hands on the baby bump.

"Aabha's quickening was too good to feel, I'll let our parents know about this right away," Shalini rushed to her phone to give this good news to her parents.

Inside Shalini's stomach, our little Aabha asked a lot of questions to herself.

"I never knew that me kicking inside over here makes my mom so happy."

"Can she feel my other movements as well?"

"My kicks, Punches?"

"Can she even feel me when I open and close my mouth and even when I suck my thumb?"

By the amount of questions she kept asking herself, she sure was a curious little lad.

***

In spite of getting good grades in the first five semesters, the next three semesters were causing Geetha a lot of trouble. With her father struggling to make both the ends meet but somehow managing to save money for her studies, Geetha still needed money for her books and personal expenses.

She decided to take up a part time job to help her father get the burden off his head. She could cover up her expenses, but what she didn't realise is that she won't have sufficient time to study. This sudden change in the allocation of time for her to study resulted in backlogs which made Geetha disappointed along with her family and the principal.

"It's the final semester now."

"Yes sir, I am aware of that."

"How are you going to defuse this situation? Did you even plan on how to bring it under control?" The principal was very curious to know why his best student isn't performing well in her exams.

"Sir, with all due respect, my family has been facing financial trouble. This drove me to take up a part time job. And hence I couldn't spare much time to study." Geetha was trying to explain the principle about all of her issues.

"Is there anything I can help you with? I can lend you some money." He wholeheartedly wanted to help Geetha.

"Sir, I really owe you for that. But I'm sorry I can't take anything from you anymore. All I would ask you to do is to provide me with suitable materials to pass my exams."

"Sure my dear. I'll do that." He gave her blessings with his whole heart and wanted to see her pursue her goals.

"Thank you sir." Geetha continued to attend her classes.

"Should I drop off from my course so I can at least save my parents' money?"

"Who would want to invest for an education full of failure and struggle?"

"Although I completed my MBBS here, my family will be nil by then and they will not be able to financially support me for my further specialization."

"It's better that I quit now and take up an assistant's job. Can't I find a couple more part time jobs to do?"

There were a lot of thoughts running up in Geetha's mind about what to do in this current situation but there were things which were holding her back and continuing her education. It was like there was this force pulling her back and not letting her go.

"After these nine semesters I even have to complete the internship to get my degree. When I can't even pass my exams, who would take me as an intern?"

"Is it better not to be a burden to my parents anymore?"

"Will it be a best option if I take up a job and start helping my family?"

"Yes it'll be, for sure I guess so."

"I don't want to fail my family again."

***

It doesn't feel good, something's not right.

"I think my water broke Midhun!" Shalini starts yelling.

Shalini had gone unconscious and she could only glimpse a few flashes where she was rushed to the hospital and the doctors started preparing her for the delivery.

"Just a few moments to go. Then I can see everyone." Aabha was so cool, although her mom can't hear her talk yet, she wanted to be there for her.

It has been a while.

Aabha's Grandparents arrived at the hospital and her dad was too tensed about her and Shalini.

The delivery was done but the doctors rushed Aabha to the NICU as there was a problem with the condition of her heart.

They kept Aabha in the ventilator and informed her parents about the situation. The doctors were not sure about how many days this condition would last.

Shalini walked to the ventilator to see Aabha and she couldn't control her emotions. She was not ready to lose another child.

***

It was seven in the evening and everything was ready for Aabha's heart surgery.

It took more than four and half hours to complete the surgery,

"I have a surprise for you," the doctor approaches Shalini and Midhun after the surgery.

"Is everything under control with our baby?" Midhun was tense.

"Yes, it is. And that's the surprise," it came as a sweet surprise to the doctor that the baby had actually survived the surgery.

"I'm sorry, but we don't understand. Can you please elaborate, doctor?" Shalini and Midhun were confused as to why the doctor was strangely happy.

The doctor then briefed them about the surgery,

"The thing is, especially for newborn babies, it's almost impossible for them to survive through such rigorous surgeries. We could only operate on her. But she survived because she is a fighter. It's rare to see babies survive like this. And the best part is that her heart is perfectly safe now and she will not have any further complications."

There was no end to those happy tears rolling out of Midhun and Shalini's eyes.

As the doctor was walking away, Aabha's grandfather called her as he wanted to have a word with her.

"Doctor!"

"Yes sir."

"What was your name again?"

"I'm Dr. Geetha, sir."

Yes. It was the same Geetha who wanted to drop off from her medical degree to help her family. It was the same Geetha who thought of taking a job instead of studying further to financially support her parents.

"There's no way to pay you back for what you have done. May God bless you with all the happiness you deserve." Aabha's grandfather finally got a granddaughter. His prayers have been answered at last.

"The doctor came in with a smile and gave that smile to us." Shalini will never ever be depressed again.

"Looking at all those happy faces, I'm glad the surgery was a success. It was worth all the effort," Geetha starts thinking to herself.

Dropping off from the course right in the middle and letting her and her parents' dreams crush inside Geetha's thoughts is not right. If at all she had quit, she wouldn't be the reason to start something today, to make Aabha live. Failing her parents and all the people around her is really something you shouldn't think about. But here as of today, achieving something which made her day, and which makes her parents proud of this is loads better than quitting. That made Geetha finish her degree and her research also helped her get a good internship, which got her a scholarship for her specialization. Was letting her parents suffer financially and mentally because of her dream is a failure? Of course not, because that day her vision was to succeed and make her parents happy. Yes, Geetha's parents struggled financially to bring her up, and now it was her turn to earn money and let them live a peaceful life.

So, where was the actual failure? It was in the idea of giving up. When all that negativity consumes you, you have to be strong enough to tackle it.

18

PAIN IS INEVITABLE BUT MISERY IS OPTIONAL

by Harshit Dudhani

"Success is walking from failure to failure with no loss of enthusiasm."

This story is of myself and how I turned my life. I was born on 14th August 1990. My name is Farooq Qureshi, my father Mr. Aftab Qureshi is a manager at Sheikh Industries and my mother Nazma Qureshi is a housewife. We stay at Mumbra near Thane. I started my schooling at Ahmed Public School when I was 4 years old. Initially, I was not able to read, write, and speak properly, so my teachers told my parents that it is common with many students and there is no need to worry. As years passed by, my problem of reading, writing, and verbalizing didn't amend so my father was very exasperated with me and he commenced beating me with instruments every other day, but my mother didn't utter a single word defending me.

When I was in 6th grade I used to watch comedy shows which made me feel blissful and helped me bear the pain that my father used to give me. It was really fun for me to watch it, but it started affecting my marks astringently and I failed in Maths and English and my overall score was 39% which was the least in the school. That day my father thrashed me for almost 2 hours as he felt mortified because he thought that everyone will laugh at him because of me, but he never tried to understand my quandary. I was bleeding a lot but then too my mother was quiet. My father thought I was a taint to him and to dispense me, he sent me to Saint Convent School, Mahabaleshwar.

I was in 7th grade and endeavoured to study a lot yet was not capable of doing it. My teachers used to penalize me, and my classmates used to laugh at me. I got demoralized and my score in that grade was only 46%. I cerebrated of committing suicide but at the same time was scared of dying. The teachers called my parents to repine them about my result. My father got frustrated and started beating me in front of everyone until my principal Mr. Krishnan Murthy intervened to save me. We went to his cabin where he visually perceived my result and asked my teachers regarding it. He concluded that I was suffering from 'DYSLEXIA' as he was a psychologist.

I was completely out of mind and my father commenced insulting me as if I had done it intentionally! But the principal explained my condition i.e. in such cases a child is not able to read words and numbers properly because they jumble the words, so they are not able to comprehend the words congruously. Teachers felt pity for me, but my father didn't try to understand what I was going through. He left the cabin with anger.

Mr. Krishnan Murthy is a gentleman, he availed me a lot. He counselled me. I told him about my social life, and he helped me to gain my confidence, though it took a year. I told him that I relished comedy shows a lot, but everyone was laughing at me because of my condition, it was then he told me that marks will never define my future, do what you love to do and don't be afraid of failure. It's a steppingstone to prosperity if you learn from it.

He motivated me to do comedy in front of my friends and later in front of the class. I tried many times but was still afraid to endeavour with a full heart because still in some corner of my heart I was in trepidation of my dad. During the initial phase of 10th grade, I endeavoured in front of the class and everyone was laughing at my japes. I was very happy, but at the same time, I was tense for my board exams. I studied a lot and somehow managed to get 61%. My father was not ecstatic with my score, so he sent me back to Saint Convent School. This time I was very jubilant while going back as I had made some good recollections during my final year in school. My father always wished that I become a medico but due to my condition of dyslexia, I took Humanities.

I still used to watch comedy shows on school computers during my free lectures and solemnly it is the best memory of my childhood. On 19th December 2006 during the last assembly before winter breaks, Mr. Murthy authoritatively mandated me to perform my comedy bit in front of the school and I was shocked, but he told me that he trusted me very much. I dared to perform in front of the school, and everyone was happy with my performance and I took a sigh of relief. After the winter break, there was an inter-school fest coming up in February so principal sir called me and asked me to perform at the fest. But this time I was confident and commenced preparing for the fest. Determinately the day came when I was going to perform in front of many colleges and this day was the best day of my life till date as everyone laughed to the fullest and everyone appreciated me.

I won the best comedian award of the fest and I was on top of the world. I acknowledged a lot to Murthy sir, and expressed my sincere gratitude towards him as the award was only possible because of his faith in me. My 12th grade commenced, and Mr. Murthy told me to now focus on my studies because this year was going to shape my career. I prepared a lot for my exams and I was very dedicated to my studies and the result too was mesmerizing because I got 70%. It was genuinely a proud moment for me, but not for my father.

I authentically missed Mr. Krishnan Murthy as he shaped my future very well; he taught me everything that would help me in life. I mentally conceived everything in my life is now perfect, but the 2008 recession transmuted my family upside down because my father lost his job, but within a month I somehow managed to get a job of washing utensils in a restaurant and they also allowed me to perform in front of their guest due to my achievement. I also managed to get admission to SJR College near Ghatkopar for my bachelor's degree in arts under minority Kota. I used to be solitary and quiet because of our financial condition.

Everyone had their groups, and no one even endeavoured to verbalize with me, and I was all alone. I gained a lot of confidence by performing at restaurants and during my second semester, I tried performing stand-up comedy in an inter-college fest and my performance was marvellous. People started interacting with me and I was enjoying my life because I made many new friends. During the second year, my father got his new job as a supervisor at Khan Industries Ltd. I mentally conceived this year would be fortuitous and our financial struggle would be over. I also gave a thought to engender a YouTube channel for stand-up comedy as YouTube was gaining popularity. Everything was going perfectly in my life, but I conjectured life is not happy with my prosperity and this time in 2010 I met with an accident where I fractured my legs, and I was given bed rest for 7 months. My morale was consummately down.

As I celebrated, life didn't want me to be jubilant but later I realized that everything in life happens for a reason, because this time my mother asked my father to at least once sanction me to live for my dreams and told him that I have suffered enough because of him and I was born to live my life, not his. I opened a YouTube channel, uploading comedy bits in 2011 but it didn't become popular for one and a half years, then I posted a different video, not of a comedy bit but this time I explained how comedy played me and my destiny.

This video became super popular and within a month my YouTube channel propagated and got heavily subscribed. My father tried to pretend that everything is normal, but as we all know the truth cannot be hidden for long and eventually I came to know about my father's liver diagnosis. I struggled a lot and tried to gain as many shows as I can perform at and I realized that from cradle to death, life is a struggle. I cleared all dues of the hospital and this time my father realized that I am capable of standing on my own feet, and he realized that he was wrong about me, he also apologized to me for everything he did to me.

After years of struggle my life was stable and my entire family was supporting me and today I am a successful You tuber and I also run an NGO for the children who don't have parents to support them as each and every kid is a genius in his own way, but “If you judge a fish on its ability to climb a tree, it will live its whole life believing that it is.

19

ILLUMINATE

by Jerry Akshita

The train arrives at the station with a whoosh at around 6 A. M, Prakash Swaminathan, a 21-year-old woke up to the buzzing "chai, chai, coffee, chai!" sounds which slurred around.

His one eye creeps open to find the chai vendor shoving a pot of tea an inch from his nose.

His refurbished Nokia-1100 rang for the 4th time, he answered abruptly, “Yes amma, I reached the Deccan Nampally station.”

Amma said, “Appa was right after all. See, he'd reserved you a berth for 8 o'clock in night, so that you reached your destination in time. C'mon, talk to him at least now.”

Prakash said, “It was you who asked me to board this berth reserved train. I'd rather boarded the 10'o clock's train by myself then.”

Amma said dejectedly, “Prakash, you definitely would've been late for your interview by 10'o clock's train.”

Prakash furiously went mad at his mother saying, romba erichall (very irritating in Tamil)

"You don't have to start lecturing me now as appa always does. He's terrible all times. He's a poor potter who barely earns a living, trying to teach me life lessons...? Have you forgotten? I am the only educated man in the entire family...uh?"

Meanwhile, Prakash rushed to the lavatory and hung the call furiously. He freshened up and changed from lungi (vesti) to formal wear. He got off the train and eventually saw 3 taxi drivers compelling amongst themselves to have Prakash as their passenger. In the midst of all this, Prakash happened to see women in concealed burkas, they only had a mesh screen to see through.

Finally, the victorious taxiwala was chewing paan, with his red-stained mouth, he swore to drive Prakash to his destination- 'The Hi-tech city'. Prakash put down his window glass to look across the similar chain of stalls on every street which were saying irani chai and biryani on them

In the wee hours of morning, roads of Hyderabad looked ravishing, the driver swiftly turned around and offered Prakash Osmania biscuits. Prakash took a glance over his luggage and tossed in some biscuits whilst his amma was ringing him up once again.

He didn't bother to pick her calls. He was overwhelmed by the Dawn chorus sung by birds and the soothing sound of azaan.

A cold shiver ran down his spine while reaching closer to the interview building-gates and in no time he highly strung, he felt taut and tense with nerves, so horrendous that even the driver could sense his awfulness. The taxi creaked along with harsh squeaking sound, taxiwala syly didn't go by the metre which turned out extravagant to Prakash. He dropped off

Prakash till the gates of interview and drove back, whimpering, “All the best thalaiva.”

Prakash offered mental prayers while nervously walking in. He looked at the passionate working women in modern attire, nevertheless, he checked his tie knot and shirt collars. On his way to the interview building He happened to see streams of water running through the ground area getting wasted. He swiftly went across and turned it off to save water. He enters the building hall and takes a look at the artistic walls and a unique vintage clock striking 8 A. M. Also showing the year 2008 on centre.

The 10 ceiling fans running for hardly 5 people in the hall concerned Prakash although very nervous, made him confront the receptionist.

“Prakash Swaminathan,” the office volunteer called his name. He breathed in deeply, exhaled and stood.

Just before the interview chamber, he saw a beautiful blue carpet with a curled edge, he straightened it properly to avoid himself and others from tripping. Cold sensations, chills ran down Prakash's spine while entering the interview-chamber. “Welcome, take your seat,” a man in an impeccable black suit spoke from his chair.

“You see, this is a hard nut to crack, we've rejected 9 people already, but you're selected, congratulations young lad. You got this job.

We were looking for highly disciplined people like you. This was a test, which you passed with flying colours, you were under CCTV surveillance from the time you entered the gates of our building,”

said the interviewer.

The news left Prakash totally flabbergasted. His mind went blank for minutes. I have been undisciplined since childhood. How come I became disciplined today?

“Appa is the one who taught me discipline over time. He went around at home lecturing me to close the running tap, to save electricity, to clean my tiny room. Although, I barely had any presence of mind in nervousness. I get it now, there came a voice subconsciously asking me to be disciplined over seeing things like these. (running tap, running ceiling fans etc),” Prakash said to himself.

Prakash lately got illuminated, he realized his arrogance and the true value of his truly strong disciplined appa as well. Prakash, who thought being lectured by his dad was obnoxious and adverse, over time it all turned out to be a true blessing in disguise.

STORY TITLE

This is your creative space. Write your own blessing in disguise and share with us on Instagram @inkfeatherspublishing.

Meet The Co-Authors

Sankalp Nanda

Sankalp has completed his post-graduation with a specialization in HR from XIMB in the year 2013. He is currently working as a Manager, HR Business Partner with Alstom. When tired of working with excel sheets, he likes putting his creativity into writing short stories and poems. He shares most of his creative work on his Instagram page @storyteller_14.

Aditi Agarwal

She's Aditi, selectively extroverted. Is busy daydreaming and obsessing over the sky. Can be found crushing over fictional characters or while listening to Taylor Swift. Will say something awkward once in a while, otherwise she's pretty awesome. You could easily find her in a crowded room, she has the most liveliest laugh. She has a thing for music, then again don't we all? Let's just say, if life was a Science Museum, she'd be the Art.

Raghavi Shankara Guhan

Raghavi is an optimistic and down-to-earth young lady currently pursuing her diploma in Biotechnology. She has a flair for arts where her hobbies and past times include dancing, singing, and writing. Known for her natural style of "play of words" and intriguing layers of subtleties created in all her stories, that keep the readers at the edge of their seat as well as connected to the storyline. All her stories are embedded with a deep sense of morals. Her humble and friendly attitude towards readers and her rare style of writing would make you all enjoy her stories without fail.

Aashreya R.

Aashreya R. is a poet, a writer, and a professional seeker of wonder in the world. She lives in the sweet noise of Hyderabad and can be found sometimes talking to flowers and at other times with her nose deep inside a book.

Archana Natarajan

Archana is a Bengaluru based blogger who likes to write in the romantic fiction and travelogue genres and is a regular contributor to Story Mirror and Indiblogger. She has also authored scientific articles as a Biochemist and is pursuing her Ph.D in Neurochemistry. Apart from blogging at http://aworldofcolors.blogspot.com and pursuing research, she also dabbles in candid wedding photography with her husband. Currently, she is busy juggling work and parenting responsibilities and is also utilizing her creative juices in compiling interesting stories that she can share with her son as he is growing up.

Aashritha Kadiri

Aashritha is a 13-year- old girl. She has a passion for reading and writing stories. Aashritha started reading since the first grade and has loved it ever since. Her other hobbies include playing tennis, basketball, bullet journaling and playing the guitar.

Anoushka Sharma

Anoushka Sharma is a seventeen-year-old, Delhi based girl. She is a writer on Wattpad and has been writing for people battling their internal battles. Anoushka has also been awarded with the "English literary award" by her school. She is a mythology enthusiast and tries to bring out the emotions of undiscovered and underrated characters. She is an actor by passion and has also been awarded "Best actor award" by DAV Committee. Anoushka strongly believes that smile solves every problem.

Prajwal Shukla

Prajwal Shukla is a prolific writing practitioner, enthusiast and has written over 440 short stories, blogs and articles on socio-economic issues and has a multitude of interests. He likes to explore conceptual fiction writing and a variety of topics in non-fiction as well.

Naqiyyah Calcuttawala

Her name is Naqiyyah and the French Culture intrigues her too much. A sucker for pretty skies who believes that one should live for small moments that often actually prove to be the light amidst the darkness and also the fact that everything is connected, and it occurs for our own good even if the situation is unbelievably adverse. Feel free to connect with her on Instagram @_naqiyyah18.

Akshaya Kosuri

Akshaya Kosuri is an avid reader, learner, writer, and a compiler. Her passion for contemporary fiction and classic literature fulfills her soul. Believing that every tiny speck of the universe has a story to tell, Akshaya weaves serenity through her words.

Apart from writing, she also enjoys travelling, volunteering, singing, anchoring, debating, and much more. Poetry for her is like illustrating with words to render emotions. Words bleed through hearts, from inked fingertips onto paper and that's what she is. Akshaya aspires to foster self-awareness and confidence through her work. You can connect with her on Instagram @the.floundering.

Malvica Sangeetham

A 20-year-old engineering student who's love for writing dates back to her high school days. For her, writing has been a reason to show a side of hers that no one could have ever imagined. She likes to make her own little fictional world as an escape from reality, and that's what gave her a nudge to write. Ask her about writing and storytelling, and she'll say, "What's the world without stories, for we are all entwined in them"!

Hitesh Kumar Singh

Being a keen lover of storytelling, be it in any form from novel to cinema, he loves to put his words onto paper. Realizing the power of imagination, he is also very much fascinated about fiction. Besides being a writer, he is an undergraduate student at Delhi University who very much admires film direction. His Instagram handle is @this_is_fiction.

Likhitha Kotika

Likhitha is a young girl who loves to tell stories. She often expresses her thoughts and feelings in her diary rather than to people. She believes that a book can be one's best companion ever both in the ways of giving one a good advice in the form of a story or listening to one's feelings without judging.

Sucharan Reddy

A confused forthright person who just divulges all of his everyday thoughts on a paper and oblige readers to it. "You can get to know absolutely anything from a 20-year-old chap" – is his motive. Writing is his part-time as his full time is confined to desi engineering.

Harshit Dudhani

Harshit Dudhani is a learner as well as a writer. He hopes that everyone finds happiness in little moments of life as well as stays away from worldly things and is happy for real. He believes that from cradle to death life is a struggle and this struggle is known as life, so enjoy it.

Deepshikha B.

B. Deepshikha Singh an 18-year-old teenager who's just a rookie in the field of writing. Her writings are mostly based on real-life events with a touch of friction. She firmly believes in optimizing and romanticizing her thoughts through her work. She also holds a special interest in poetry and couplets. Apart from being glued to her writing skills, she's also a sports enthusiast and has been a part of many tournaments including horse riding, kabaddi, rock climbing, and track field. She is also a melomaniac and a self-trained keyboard player. She can be contacted at: lightyagimi1623@gmail.com

Jerry Akshita

Jerry Akshita is a 17-year-old Medical Aspirant from Hyderabad, who doesn't believe clinging alone to academics would nourish over-all development. She loves doing co-curricular activities. She believes in learning piece of something from everything. She believes having love for learning is important. She's into writing for the first time to give her reflection of thoughts. Every individual would learn something different from her titled Story- 'Illuminate'. This story will enable you to think over your Basic core values. As in this fast-changing lifestyle, We are bound to change but what remains us is our strong-core values. You can connect with her on Instagram @jerry_akshita.

Lakshmi Sai Kumar

A 19-year-old management student who prefer actions over words. Lakshmi Sai Kumar believes that life is nothing but an opportunity with various outcomes and in the end, life is what you make out of it. He is a practical person who takes rational approach and trying to express his feelings through writing as He believe that books change lives.

INKFEATHERS PUBLISHING

India's Most Author Friendly Publishing House

Stay updated about latest books, anthologies, events, exclusive offers, contests, product giveaways and other things that we do to support authors.

Inkfeathers Publishing

@InkfeathersPublishing

@_Inkfeathers

@Inkfeathers

Inkfeathers.com

We'd love to connect with you!